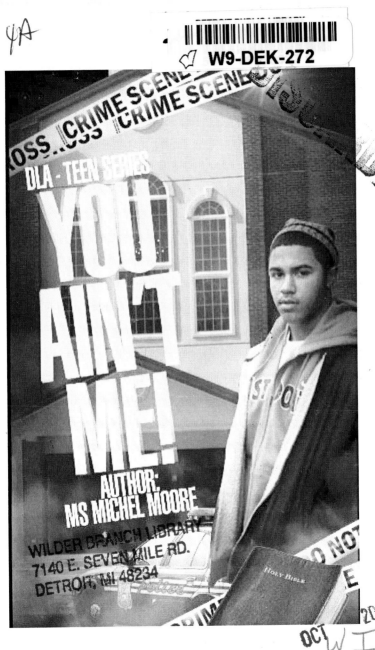

DLA - TEEN SERIES

YOU AIN'T ME!

AUTHOR:
MS MICHEL MOORE

You Ain't Me!

By Ms Michel Moore

You Ain't Me! © 2011 Michel Moore

First Print- September2011

ISBN-09769991-8-8

Say U Promise Publications
    PO. Box 38162
Detroit, Michigan 48238
   sayupromise@hotmail.com

Cover Art; JayLee Hustle
Cover Model; Dawson Fletcher
            TheJuicer_18

This novel is a work of fiction. It is not meant to portray or depict ant real persons, living or dead. Any references to locales and events are a product of the Ms. Moore's vivid and colorful imagination.

This, along with future **DLA-Teen** releases,
is dedicated to kids born, raised or living in *The Hood*.
YOU ARE SOMEBODY!

Chapter One

"How could this have happened? My son never did anything to anyone. That fool that shot him is gonna pay!" In route to the hospital, Tosha Renee Mills was trembling with every word she spoke. "I mean it. My baby is a good boy!"

Having run every red light as soon as she got the frantic call from her neighbor, she swerved up in her brand new expensive truck. Not caring about the uniformed security guard pointing to the no standing sign, defiant she blocked the Trauma Room entrance of the hospital anyway. Abandoning her Aunt to turn the engine off and legally park, Tosha, hysterical, jumped down from the vehicle running through the door just as her injured son was being unloaded from the ambulance.

"Quick-hurry, bring him into trauma room four!" The emergency unit nurse motioned to the paramedics as she ran alongside the stretcher with Tosha close behind. "A team of doctors are already waiting-hurry!"

"His pulse is dropping rapidly and we can't get a heartbeat!" one of the paramedics responded back with extreme urgency. As his rubber gloves shook, full of clotting blood, knowing their young gunshot victim was clinging to life he started to sweat. "It's getting worse. Y'all better hurry! It ain't looking good; he's bleeding out-he's bleeding out!"

Little Ro was moaning in pain. The inside pit of his stomach was burning and he couldn't open his eyes. He couldn't seem to breathe. He couldn't move his legs. He tried, but just couldn't. Suddenly his arm went limp and fell to the side of the stretcher causing everyone to panic even more, especially his mother.

"Oh naw! Oh my God!" Tosha's diamond tennis bracelet Little Ro had just blessed her with a few days before sparkled underneath the Emergency Room bright lights as she screamed out in painful denial. "Oh my God!" It was almost more than she could take watching her teenage son seem to be losing his battle to see another sunrise. "Please help him! Please! Please! He's just a baby! Come on y'all help him! Help him! Do something!" she ear splittingly demanded.

"I'm sorry, but you can't go back there," the grey haired nurse, sympathetic in tone, held up both hands. "Wait a minute!" Stopping the anguished Tosha dead in her tracks at the swinging metal double doors that led to the Triage Area, the nurse was still hopeful. "Don't worry Miss. He's in good hands. And just as soon as we know something, one of the doctors will be right out to speak with you," she assured the teen's mother.

"Why did this happen?" Tosha hyperventilated as her sobs echoed loudly throughout the walls of the crowded building. Holding her chest, Tosha panted in an attempt to catch her breath. Out of nowhere the frantic mother collapsed into her Aunt's arms that'd just come inside the building. With her new *Coach* purse swinging from her shoulder, dressed in tight jeans and stiletto pumps, she was close to blacking out entirely. "Why? Why is this happening to my baby?" Tosha cried repeatedly wishing she'd never let her son, Little Ro, sell drugs to pay the bills and help feed the family.

"Tosha! Stop it! Hush!"

"Naw Auntie, I swear, if I could turn back the hands of time, I'd trade all the shopping sprees, trips to the casino, this jewelry I'm rocking," she snatched her gold chain off her neck throwing it to the ground in desperation. "And that new Range Rover I'm driving- all back in if I could only have my baby boy in one piece, not lying back there with two big bullet holes in his body!"

Auntie Bell sat in the dreary and drab decorated hospital waiting room clutching her Bible. Opening her purse, she wiped away her distraught nieces' tears with an old tattered handkerchief she kept tucked in the side pocket. After somewhat calming her, she suggested to Tosha she try taking it down a notch or two. "Everyone's looking at you child! I know you worried but, please!"

"What!" Tosha shouted, poked out her lips and sucked her teeth. "I don't care if they look at me to their eyes fall out they head, I'ma shut up when I want to! That's my son back there all shot up fighting for his life- not theirs!" Tosha mean mugged everyone sitting near her including her Aunt. Still breathing hard from rushing to get to the hospital, Tosha resembled a raccoon as her eyeliner dripped down her face along with her tears.

"Even at my age," Auntie Bell quietly reflected handing Tosha her bible, "It's simply amazing to me how things can go plum berserk so quickly. I mean one minute you're riding sky high on top of your game, and then within a momentary blink of the eye, your soul is practically scraping the ungodly rock bottom of this wretched earth."

"Dang, will you please stop with all that church talk?" the weeping Tosha shoved the black leather book back into her Aunt's hands as she anxiously awaited any news about her oldest child who was just yards away with two gunshot holes in his chest the size of golf balls. "Little Ro might die back there and you out here trying to take me to church! Old woman bye! Kick rocks!" Tosha stopped crying long enough to give her Auntie the hand.

"Now stop all that hand mess y'all young folk be doing and all that noise! Just stop it!" Auntie Bell hated that she was getting so frustrated with her niece's showing out, but surely Tosha didn't need God or anybody else to reveal to her all the reasons behind Little Ro getting shot. It was no big secret. Plain and simple,

Auntie Bell blamed Tosha. "Now tell me, Sweetie, was all that rotten blood soiled drug money your first born showered you with worth it? You running around town buying this and that acting like a Ghetto Princess, was it all worth it?"

Tosha sniffed wiping her face and didn't hesitate to respond, "No, of course not, but why in the world is God doing this to my baby? Making him suffer?" Tosha questioned, looking up toward the ceiling, arms folded as she rocked back and forth. "I know I was wrong to keep letting him sling those pills, but the money he was making day after day was so good!" Tosha's tone was cynical as she moved her long blonde streaked sew in weave out her face.

"God?" Auntie Bell questioned.

"Here we go! -Yeah, if you wanna keep it a hundred and wanna blame someone so bad for what my boy and me done suffered through the last few years, you can blame God or maybe that no good Sean and his crackhead mother Salena! Little Ro's daddy got murdered messing around with them low lives. I should have known better than to let that troublemaking hooligan in my house! Now how about that Auntie?"

"Tosha! You best hush up that mouth of yours questioning the Lord! Don't you dare blame him for this awful tragedy!" Auntie Bell jumped to her feet shaking her finger at her disrespectful niece. "This is entirely your fault Tosha Mills, not the man upstairs or those other folk Little Ro was running these Detroit streets dealing drugs with! Now what you need to do, instead of flapping that smart mouth of yours, is think back to the role you done played in Little Ro turning out the way he is!" the old woman let her have it raw and uncut as the other people in the waiting room listened shaking their heads. "Truth be told, you might as well have pulled the trigger of that gun yourself! Now Miss I'm The Stuff, how's about that for keeping it real and as you say- a hundred?"

Pissed, wanting nothing more than to curse her old sassy talking Aunt out, Tosha sat speechless at her hurtful words and accusations. Yet, as her mind wondered back over the past couple of years, she couldn't help but questioned whether or not her aunt's words might have held some truth. Maybe she did put too much pressure on Little Ro to step up to the plate after his daddy got killed. *Was I that selfish? Did I make my son sell drugs so I could live good? Dang what did I do? Maybe it was my fault he got shot.*

Closing her eyes tightly scratching her head, Tosha got chills as she thought back to where she might've gone wrong raising Little Ro.

Chapter Two

Five short years earlier...

"Little Ro, call your father and tell him dinner will be ready in about twenty minutes or so," Tosha ordered her son wiping her hands on a dish towel. "Oh, and tell him I cooked his favorite, fried chicken, sweet corn, collards, biscuits and gravy."

"Okay, Ma, I will," the eldest of Tosha Mills two children sighed, answering back as he stood over his little sister Janai, making sure she washed her face and hands before sitting down at the dinner table.

"Oh, and please tell him to try and not be too late either."

Roland Dean Mills Jr. was only twelve years old, but shouldered a great deal of responsibility for a boy of his age. Being the namesake of a stern but fair father was sometimes more than the rambunctious youngster could handle, yet he never wanted to disappoint the man he deemed as his time to time hero. Unlike most of his classmates, his parents were still married living under the same roof. Even with the arguments and disagreements about any and everything, they stuck it out. Although, truth be told, making the usual shameful call night after night summoning his dad home supposedly from his *'boy's house'* for his mother was fast becoming a habit that was growing old with Little Ro.

"Hello Daddy?"

"Hey now Little Ro, is your mom's dinner ready yet?"

"Yes Daddy and she said don't be late!"

"Okay, I'll be there in a few. Tell her I said to keep the food hot."

Each evening before Little Ro went to sleep, he prayed his mother would get the courage to stand up for herself and stop being his father's constant doormat. He knew she deserved much better than how his overbearing father was playing her.

God, please give my Momma strength to stop Daddy from going over to that nasty, stank looking lady's house all the time. I hate her and her dumb-dumb son Sean that gets to see him as much as me and Janai do. Amen!

The man of the house, Roland Sr. worked the early morning shift at General Motors on the line. He was a tall muscular man in statue that everyone in his close knitted block on the west side of Detroit knew. Highly regarded wherever he went, whether it was out of fear of his quick fire temper or just plain respect, the father of two was a force to be reckoned with.

You Ain't Me!

Migrating from Alabama in the eighties, Roland Sr. had a swagger and southern charm that made him the perfect gentleman to most.

For those strangers who didn't know any better, from the outside looking in, Tosha was indeed blessed with a perfect man. It was true, omitting the common knowledge to those living near the couple, that he was involved in an ongoing affair with Salena Jackson. She was a single mother of one, who'd recently moved into the area and was quickly known as the neighborhood *good time girl* who slept with just about anything that hopped, skipped or jumped as long as they paid her.

Taking that one negative and outrageous factor out the equation, the head of household, Roland Sr. rarely missed a meal with his own family. He was a good paymaster; never late on one bill that crossed the modest threshold of their brick framed bungalow home. Not causing his wife to worry about the high mortgage, food in the cabinets or clothes on the kid's backs, Roland Sr. thought his blatant indiscretions and the sideway glances of pity his spouse endured from neighbors were somehow allowable. Whenever his wife came in the house embarrassed and ashamed of what people would say out loud as well as whisper about his cheating ways, Roland Sr. would buy her a dozen roses or maybe treat Tosha to a brand new dress to soothe her pain.

"Did you call him?" Tosha asked her son a few minutes later after giving him the order to originally call his father to dinner.

"Yes, Ma, I called." Little Ro secretly rolled his eyes at her stupidity of dealing with his daddy and all his madness.

"And is he on his way?" Tosha wondered as she set the table then rinsed out a few glasses. "I don't want his dinner to get cold."

"Do you want me to go and get him from around the corner- I can?" Receiving a cold hard stare from his mother, Little Ro instantly regretted asking her that million dollar question, but couldn't help himself as he headed towards the front door. "I know what house she stays in. It's not a problem."

"What did you just say to me?" Tosha, with wet hands, slowly approached her son with a look of venom in her eyes as Janai watched scared that her brother was seconds away from getting popped right in the mouth.

"Nothing Ma." He wisely backed down, treading on dangerous ground, wanting to avoid trouble. "I didn't say nothing."

"I thought not." She angrily wiped her hands down her apron. In just those few seconds, her blood had boiled just enough to form a bead of sweat across her forehead. "You ain't so big that you can't get a whooping. Now go sit your wanna be grown behind on that front porch and let me know the minute your father pulls up. You understand me?"

"Yes Ma. I understand." Little Ro twisted his lip up as he thought about how his father was disrespecting his mom every single day. *I wish he'd go away and never come back!*

Tosha, five foot three with a paper bag brown skin tone and shoulder length hair, took pride in being a good person. The thirty-four year old mother stayed immersed in helping the kids with their homework and volunteering at the church when she could. Keeping busy, she hid from the reality that faced her daily as the nosey women in her neighborhood made it their personal vendetta to give Tosha their jaded opinion on her husbands' extra martial dealings. Although most claimed they were just trying to help her or put her up on game, Tosha wasn't a fool, by no means. She knew they were just trying to be all up in her business and refused to give them the satisfaction of knowing how hurt she truly was.

For better or worse, richer or poorer, was Tosha's constant response to the women, while trying to hold her head up and keep her dignity intact. *One day Salena Jackson gonna get hers, y'all see!*

Unfortunately, Tosha Mills wasn't the only one who suffered the shame from her husbands' constant cheating. Little Ro would catch it, going to the corner store, at the playground and even in the lunchroom line. Ridiculed by his classmates for having a *'play step brother'* Sean Jackson who was in the slow class, he tried his best to ignore the taunts. However sadly, he stayed in detention as a result of physical retaliation, disappointing his parents. Little Ro couldn't help but try to beat down anyone of the other kids for talking smack about how dumb his mother was for staying married to his no good daddy. Little Ro didn't want to fight, but it was the point and principal, even though deep down inside he knew his classmates were right.

As Little Ro did as he was told by his mother sitting silently on the wood steps looking back and forth up the block for more than twenty minutes, he grew inpatient awaiting any sign of his father. Just when he thought he'd die from hunger, Roland Sr.'s two toned pickup truck turned the corner, roaring into the driveway.

"Hey, Pops. You know you're late," Little Ro sarcastically pointed out to his father as he hopped out of the truck and made his way to the porch.

"Yeah I know, so come on and let's eat," Roland Sr. stated nonchalantly as he rested his hand on his son's shoulder and they entered the house. They both walked into the dining room at the same time. "I'm starving Tosha! I could eat a horse!" Roland Sr. smiled as the smell of the delicious foods assaulted his nose.

"I thought I told you to tell me when he pulled up?" Tosha tugged her son's earlobe.

"Sorry Ma. I forgot." Little Ro found his spot at the table across from Janai.

"What's the big deal, Tosha?" Roland Sr. stated after witnessing his son's upbeat demeanor take a dismal change. "Just relax."

"He's always forgetting something lately." Tosha judgmentally raised her eyebrow. It was obvious that she was more disappointed in her husband's tardiness versus her son's forgetfulness. Caught in her emotions, her eyes dared her husband to call her on it as she turned to retrieve the pan of homemade biscuits from the warm oven.

"Listen here, Tosha. I'm not in the mood to hear all that nerve wrecking complaining you doing," Roland Sr. scolded his wife as if she was a child. "That's why I stay away most of the time-that fly mouth of yours!"

"Roland!" she turned with the platter of hot biscuits in her hands. "Have you lost your mind? Don't say that in front of my kids!"

"I know you not telling me what to say in my own house are you?"

"No but I-"

"But nothing!" he insisted as he sat down at the head of the table. "Just bring me my plate so I can eat, take a hot shower and go to bed! I'm tired!"

Tosha, always the one to back down to her bossy husband, decided to let him win this time also. Preparing her family's plates she sat down, joining her husband, son and daughter at the dinner table. As the family lowered their heads, Roland Sr., who was the biggest hypocrite in the room, led them in a prayer before the family dug in, devouring almost every dish Tosha had lovingly prepared. First the fried chicken disappeared, then all the greens followed by the corn.

Inhaling the aroma of a fresh hot apple pie warming in the oven, the troubled husband and wife went through the normal ritual of idle chit chat.

"So how was your day?" Tosha asked Roland Sr. trying to stay on his good side.

"Same as it always is, Tosha," he huffed while pouring honey on the last piece of bread. "Long and drawn out. I swear if I didn't have you and these kids that always need something or another; I'd quit that factory and let some other fool have that headache job!"

"Babe, just be blessed you have steady work as bad as the economy is."

"What you know about the economy? You ain't got no worries!" He barely looked over to acknowledge her, "You living real good around here as far as I can see!"

"That's not necessarily true. It's getting harder by the day to stretch the food budget on these two," she said matter of fact ally, watching her son and daughter drink their glasses of grape Kool-Aid. "And they say times are about to get much harder."

Roland Sr. fingers, sticky and crumbs around his mouth, glanced upwards from his plate. "Tosha, are you saying I don't give you enough to provide for my children? Are you saying I don't work hard enough in that sweat box day after day?" Roland Sr. was now on the defensive side as his voice got louder.

"No Roland, I was just saying the prices at the grocery store are going up." She once again backed down, fearing her man's harsh verbal tongue lashing would increase in tone. "That's all."

Little Ro and Janai, his sister, were used to the mental abuse their mother was forced to undergo and knew to just be quiet and stay out of grown folks business as they were reminded constantly.

"Can you tell me, why do you always find something to get on my back about?" Roland Sr. asked his wife with a slight pound on the dinner table causing the pitcher of Kool-Aid to rattle. "I'm out there every day busting my butt and all you do is sit around and constantly complain. If you don't appreciate me then…"

"Then what? Humph! I guess that sleazy Salena you keep chasing behind is perfect, huh?" Tosha mumbled under her breath as if she was second guessing even making the comment in the first place.

You could've heard a pin drop around the table as Roland Sr. let his fork fall onto the plate, giving Tosha a wicked crooked grin. "What did you just say?"

Tosha took a deep breath before speaking. "You heard me, Roland!" she raised her usually timid voice, getting up out of her chair showing she wasn't in the mood for any more of his bully routine. She didn't know where this sudden burst of courage, or holy boldness as the women in the church would have called it, came from, but she was going to use it up while it lasted. "I do my best to make you and this family happy, and all I get in return is grief! I'm tired of being second best! You gonna get rid of that home wrecker Salena once and for all and I mean it!"

Roland Sr. sat dumbfounded at a loss for words. His wife had never called him out on his behavior before. And now, after seeing the hurt in her eyes and hearing the pain in her voice, he almost felt bad for messing around behind her back. He finally conjured up some words to speak, but before Roland Sr. could respond or reassure his wife of his half time devotion to her, his cell phone rang interrupting the spontaneous argument.

Taking his Blackberry off his thick leather belt, Roland Sr. looked at the screen and saw Salena's number flash repeatedly. Confused for the reason she was calling him at this time of the evening, knowing good and well he was having dinner with Tosha and the kids, Roland Sr. disrespectfully pushed the talk button as his family listened in on the one sided conversation.

"Yeah!...What?...He did what?...Why is he even over there?...Is he touching you?...I'm on my way!" Roland Sr. leaped to his feet, grabbing his truck keys and almost knocking his small daughter out of her seat.

"Have you lost your mind, Roland? Where do you think you are going right in the middle of dinner?" Tosha couldn't believe her eyes and ears as she and her two children followed her irate husband onto the front porch, watching him jump in his truck. "Roland!" Tosha irately called out. "You get back in here with your family right now! This is ridiculous! Enough is enough! I swear!"

"Tosha, y'all go back inside the house and finishing eating!" Roland Sr. yelled as the nosey neighbors watched. "This doesn't concern you or my kids!" He quickly backed out the driveway and was on his way back down the street in the same direction he had come from just less than a half hour prior.

Having no choice but to do as they were instructed, Tosha ushered Little Ro and her young daughter off the porch and back into their home. Hours seemed to pass as the evening sunlight disappeared, making way for the glow of the moon. The kids had long since gone to bed as Tosha, who sat on the couch furiously awaiting Roland Sr.'s return, simmered.

I'm done! If he wants to be with that hoodrat so bad, he can have her! *I'm done!* Tosha told herself, knowing deep in her heart though; she didn't want to lose her family just that easy. She closed her weary eyes for what seemed to only be a few seconds, but was suddenly startled by the loud sounds of the telephone. *Oh, now I guess he wants to call with some sort of an excuse before he pulls up. I wonder what lie he's gonna tell this time!* The angry wife recognized her husband's number on the caller I.D. and answered dryly.

"Yes, Roland."

"Hello, Tosha?"

A puzzle look instantly came across Tosha's face. Although she was certain it was her husband's phone number that appeared on the caller ID, the voice speaking on the other end of the line was clearly not that of Roland Sr.'s.

"Yes, this is Tosha." She paused, momentarily shocked at not hearing his voice on the other end. "Who is this?"

"This is Salena." The woman's voice sounded grim.

"Salena?... Salena Jackson? You have some nerve-" Tosha shouted into the receiver before she was cut off.

"Tosha, wait, please. It's an emergency!" Salena begged.

"Oh, I bet. Well you can take your emergency to 911, sweetheart, but don't call my house-"

Once again, Salena cut her off. "Tosha wait- just listen and don't hang up! Please!"

"How dare you! You've got some sort of nerve calling my house. Haven't you disrespected me and my children enough over this past year?"

"Please, Tosha, just listen to me!" This time Salena shouted out with authority and Tosha could tell at that point something strange was going on. "There's been an accident."

"Why are you calling me on my husbands' phone? Where is he? Put him on the line." As she became nervous by the seriousness of the female caller's voice, Tosha fired question after question out to her husband's long time Mistress.

"That's what I'm trying to tell you." Salena started crying uncontrollably. "Roland's been hurt and the paramedics are putting him in the ambulance as we speak. He's on his way to the hospital. He's asking for you. You'd better hurry!"

"What?" Tosha yelled, waking Little Ro up out of a deep sleep. "Oh my God, what kind of accident was my husband in? Where are they taking him- to what hospital?"

"I don't know! I don't know! But it looks really bad!" Salena's tears increased. "It's so much blood!" She made the last statement as if she was looking at the blood as she spoke.

The fact that Tosha hadn't appreciated Salena calling her one little bit, now had to be put on the back burner as she dropped the phone to the floor and ran to get her purse. "Baby I'll be back! Watch your sister and lock the door- your father is hurt!"

Little Ro, now out the bed standing in the doorway, wiped the sleep out his eyes watching his mother leave, rushing off to the hospital. Fighting the tears back, somehow he knew he'd never see his father alive again and his young life would be forever changed.

Chapter Three

The funeral was long and grueling for the many grieving relatives. Person after person got up to praise the deceased Roland Mills Sr. for his past various deeds and work throughout the community. Finding no comfort in becoming a widow with two young children to bring up in the wicked streets of Detroit, thanks to one of Salena Jackson's many boyfriends that had cold bloodedly shot her husband four times murdering him in a jealous rage, Tosha hid her face in her hands. As the service concluded and they rolled her man's silver and grey trimmed casket out the same church they exchanged vows at years earlier, she sobbed.

Right before climbing into the back of the family car, Little Ro, dressed in a dark blue suit, couldn't help but take notice of Ms. Jackson and her son, Sean, a.k.a., his *play step brother,* standing amongst the multitude of tearful mourners. It was rumored throughout the neighborhood and school, that Sean, the same age as Little Ro, unfortunately had witnessed the entire murder take place and was the one to place the initial call to 911.

When Tosha became aware of their uninvited presence, she wiped her red, puffy eyes, took a deep breath and confidently marched over to Salena while holding her Bible close to her breast. With the stunned crowd of family members and friends looking on, the young widow gave the little boy a faint smile then directed her full attention to his mother. Raising her hand, she landed a well place smack across Salena's face.

Tosha, furious, shook with every word she began to speak to the woman through her clenched teeth. "How dare you! Not even on this one day can you respect the union of our marriage. You got some nerve showing up here!"

Salena, embarrassed, just stood there silently holding her stinging face with one hand and Sean's with the other as Tosha continued to spit her venom.

"You don't belong here. I don't care how you felt about *my* husband. You need to know that he never loved you! Never! I was his wife- not you!" With malice, she held up her hand showing her wedding band. "Turn around and look!" Tosha pointed to Little Ro and a crying Janai, whom were off to the side holding hands, together mourning the loss of their father. "Do you see my kids standing over there?" she angrily waved her finger. "Thanks to you they don't have a father anymore. Are you happy? You're nothing but a home

wrecking skank and I hope all the wives standing around here watch their husbands whenever you around! You lucky I don't do more than just slap you!" Tosha shot Salena one last long glare before saying, "You's a snake and trust one day you gonna catch it!"

With that being said, Tosha's family members ushered her to the long dark colored sedan so they could start the lengthy procession to the cemetery, which was located across town. Each of the women in attendance whispered amongst their selves, thinking that they could have easily been in Tosha's shoes. Tightly they held onto their husbands arms as they snarled walking pass a humiliated Salena Jackson who was still subconsciously holding the side of her face and her young son's hand.

*****

After Roland Sr. was buried and all was said and done, and the reality of living set in, Tosha came to find out exactly where she and her children basically stood. Roland Sr. had left his wife with several high credit card balances, one huge water bill and of course the mortgage. Even though she cashed in a seventy-five hundred dollar insurance policy, which mostly went to cover burial expenses, she was almost flat broke. Having no other choice but to provide for Little Ro and Janai, Tosha took a job at a small factory. She knew if they all didn't pull it together, they'd be out in the streets or living with one of her relatives, which for her was definitely not an option.

"Little Ro, can you help me fix the eggs while I get your sister dressed to go to Auntie Bell's. I'm running kinda late," Tosha ordered her son, who was now looked upon as the man of the house. "Thanks, I appreciate it."

"Not a problem, Ma. I got you!"

"Oh yeah, I left that seven dollars you needed for a new gas container over there on the table." Tosha rushed through the house getting ready for her shift.

"Okay, I'll get it as soon as I get finish with this," Little Ro said as he began to prepare a skillet of scrambled cheese eggs.

After putting plenty of eggs on two plates for his sister and mother, Little Ro scraped the last bit out the black cast iron skillet onto his own plate. "I've got three yards to do today," he shouted out to his mom as he walked over to the kitchen table and sat down.

"That's good, baby!" Tosha yelled back into the kitchen to her hard working son.

For the past four years since her husbands' untimely death, Little Ro had assumed the role of the man of the house by taking on odd jobs in order to be able to contribute to the household bills. Those years had been harder than Tosha could have ever imagined. At some points, she grew so weary that she would lose hope. Each day in the single mother's life caused her to change for the worse as the bill collectors kept calling demanding payments and the shut off notices piled up.

As the days drug by, Tosha Mills, who'd easily gained thirty pounds over the course of the last four years began sipping on more than just a small glass of wine with dinner. She seemed to get spiteful and judgmental, blaming Salena Jackson and her small son for taking away her husband. As the months flew by, her anger increased and so did her bad attitude. Tosha needed a crutch to lean on so it was second nature for her to depend on the only man in her life, Roland Jr. whether he was ready for that responsibility or not.

In between Little Ro cutting grass, shoveling snow in the winter months and staying on the honor roll at high school he took care of his younger sister, Janai. The always busy teen was faced with obstacle after obstacle. When the new Air Jordan's came out, of course he couldn't get a pair. Spending money on a fitted cap every week like some of his classmates did was also out the question. Designer track suits, expensive jeans or new games for a used X-Box he and his sister shared, Little Ro knew better than to even dream about it. They weren't in the family's strict budget.

Things with his household's financial situation were looking more than dismal the sunny afternoon he walked up to his loyal customer Lamont's two story home.

Anytime he would cut Lamont's lawn or trim the hedges, he never needed to bring his own equipment. Lamont, a local drug dealer, had everything Little Ro required in a shed located in the rear of the huge fenced in backyard. Lamont wasn't like the average dope dealer in the movies, callous and demented with no use for anyone other than himself. He used to sit on the back deck reading books to his small son as Little Ro cut the grass. Lamont also coached football for the Children's League.

Even though Little Ro didn't necessarily condone Lamont's over the top lifestyle and the way he made his living, he still understood the hustle and the grind. Life was hard in Detroit and whatever someone felt they were forced to do to survive and feed their families was understandable, even if it was illegal.

Noticeably this day was different from most as Little Ro neared the front porch as he did every two weeks. Outside of all the strange cars parked in the driveway, something else seemed out of the ordinary to Little Ro. Even though Lamont knew a lot of people in and around the city, he never had this much company at his house at one time. The few occasions that he did see any of Lamont's cronies, they were all pushing hotter whips than the ones that were now parked on the premises. It was like a used car parade on display.

"Um yes, can I help you?"

Little Ro was rudely met by a middle aged woman with a pile of men's clothes gathered in her arms.

"What do you want?" the woman firmly asked as if she was getting impatient with him for taking too long to reply.

"I'm here to do the yard work. Is Lamont home?"

"Naw, he ain't here, so don't be expecting no money for nothing or no handouts!"

"Oh, he already took care of me, so it's all good." Lamont always paid him for the entire month up front so even by chance if he wasn't at home, the job would still be taken care of without Little Ro wondering when he'd get his money. Hearing loud voices, Little Ro tried to inconspicuously play it off and look over the woman's shoulder. He was more than curious as to what all the noise and commotion coming from the inside of Lamont's usually quiet home was about. "I come every two weeks," Little Ro added still trying to investigate low key.

Looking down at the growing grass then back over at the people inside, who were getting more boisterous as the seconds passed, the woman finally told Little Ro to go ahead, cut the yard and leave her alone. "Look- I tell you what, this is my house now anyway and I don't want it looking a hot mess! So, yeah go ahead and do your thing! And hurry up!"

"Your house - over my dead body!" One man holding a small box of what appeared to be DVD's yelled out the doorway.

"Mine too!" A female added her two cent. "He would've wanted me to have this house and that flat screen! I was his favorite cousin and y'all all know that!"

What are they talking about...their house? When Lamont shows up he's gonna trip out on all these loud crazy people up in his crib. Slowly heading to the rear of the house, a confused Little Ro saw Lamont's baby momma, Tanika, and five year old son pull up. Jumping out the car, Tanika appeared to be infuriated. *Good here comes Nika!* Little Ro knew Lamont's son's mother was no joke. Everyone had heard the stories of her practically beating down any females from around the way that even considered trying to get with 'her man'.

"Hey! How y'all gonna be all up in the house like it belongs to y'all?" Tanika huffed as she made her way up to the door, dragging her son by the hand the entire way.

"Girl- bye." The woman who had been so rude to Little Ro was being just as rude to Tanika. "This here is family business and don't concern you at all! You acting like you were his wife!"

"Well, this is his son, his blood, so that makes it my business!" Tanika, with tears forming in her eyes, screamed back at the woman as she held onto her son.

By now several people came out of the house and began to congregate in the front yard. One by one, like tiny ants, they started loading clothes, shoes, televisions and just about anything else they could carry from Lamont's home into their hoopties.

"Listen here, Ms. Thang- with ya uppity behind," one other person spoke up. "Real Talk; unless you got papers to this or that", she pointed around then planted her hands firmly on her hips, "then you need to step. Lamont was our relative, so that gives us first grabs at everything in and around here!"

"Y'all so disrespectful it don't make no sense." Tanika, now crying, shook her head in disgust. "He hasn't even been dead twenty-four hours and y'all over here behaving like a pack of wild vultures!"

Lamont's son started to cry as his mother shouted at his cousins, aunts and uncles. "He couldn't stand none of y'all when he was alive, so what makes y'all think he'd want y'all to have anything of his?"

"Oh well! He ain't here to answer that himself now is he?" a cousin smartly replied as she carried three leather jackets in tow even though it was the beginning of summer. She then laughed placing them inside of her opened trunk. "Stop being a hater Tanika, you done got yours from my big cousin when he was alive, now we getting ours!"

"Yeah!" another supposed relative cosigned holding a microwave. "And anyway, what in the hell is you doing here anyway? You and that illegitimate baby of yours live clean across town. Obviously you just mad we beat you to the punch."

There was more laughter among several of Lamont's family members at Tanika's expense.

"Unlike all of you desperate bums," Tanika grieved with puffy red eyes, "I've got keys to this house and the property inside that belongs to me! Y'all scrubs over here stealing from a dead man instead of mourning his loss! Y'all off the hook!"

Frozen in his tracks, Little Ro realized that Lamont was just not home for the time being, but that he was dead. Getting a hard knot in the pit of his stomach, Little Ro leaned against the concrete wall in denial. Since his father's death, Lamont was now the closes person to Little Ro that had passed away. Even though they weren't homeboys or running partners, Little Ro and Lamont had a mutual respect for one another and he would definitely miss their bi-monthly chats.

Dang, I wonder what happened? Ah naw! Little Ro let his emotions take over as he closed his eyes thinking about why people had to die, especially so young. *Life ain't fair.*

Finally, after regaining his composure, Little Ro went into the medium size shed and pulled out the lawn mower. Lamont had paid him to do a job, and even though he wasn't gonna be there on the back porch making him laugh, he still knew that he wanted to cut the grass one more time to fulfill his obligation. As the loud sounds of the mower ripped through the yard, Little Ro couldn't help overhear the shouts, screams and apparent smashing up of items from inside the house.

While trimming the hedges, Little Ro sadly noticed Lamont's small son, who'd somehow wondered out the house and was standing near the curb.

"What's going on, Lil' Man?" he questioned the child.

"Nuttin'," the boy shrugged.

"Tired of all the big people making noise, huh?"

"Yes." He covered his ears, which were big just like his now deceased father's. "And I want my Daddy!"

Before Little Ro could console the small boy any further, remembering exactly how he felt the day his own father passed, Tanika barreled out the front door with an arm full of her and her son's belongings that thankfully weren't gangstered by Lamont's ill mannered kin folk. Tossing the stuff in the rear of the car, Tanika looked over at her son who stared down toward the pavement to keep from crying.

"Come on baby, let's go before Mommy messes around and catches a murder case!" She snatched the distraught boy up by the arm, practically throwing him into the passenger seat, not even bothering to safely strap him in.

"You best get on!" one cousin yelled from the porch, watching Tanika roar off the block, which was now crowed with onlookers from the neighborhood who'd gotten the word Lamont had been killed the night before.

Little Ro was pissed off to the eighth degree as he marched in the back yard grabbing a broom to clean up before he left the premises for what he knew would certainly be the last time. When the teen was almost ready to leave, the same woman he'd first encountered when he'd arrived came out onto the back deck and walked out into the middle of the freshly cut grass. After seeming to survey his work she called him over.

"Listen here," she frowned. "I want you to take that lawnmower and all the rest of that stuff out that shed and off my property! Do you understand?"

"Excuse me, Miss?" Little Ro wanted to honestly smack the cow mess outta the rude woman, but was always taught to respect his elders, so he held his composure. "I don't understand what you mean."

"Everything ain't always meant for you to understand!" She placed her hands on her wide oversized hips. "That ugly shack is blocking the place where my new gazebo gonna go! Now is you gonna clean it out and take all that junk with you, or do you want me to flag down one of these guys out here scraping? Which one is it gonna be?"

With a brief moment of hesitation, Little Ro happily headed over to the shed gathering as much of his newly acquired lawn equipment he could onto a steel push cart. *Thanks Lamont, I know this is a blessing from you.* Snatching a royal blue tarp off the ground that was thrown in the corner, he noticed something strange. Leaning over to inspect what seemed to be hidden in a cardboard box, Little Ro couldn't believe his eyes as he crotched down. Even though he was raised in the church before his father died and avoided the street life that tempted him on a daily basis, Little Ro recognized what most would called a gift from the good man upstairs.

What in th...? Little Ro puzzled to himself as he glanced over his shoulder to see if the woman had returned outside to check on rather he was gone or not. *I must be dreaming. I gotta be!*

As he peeked into the small sized duffle bag which had a broken zipper, he pulled out a manila colored envelope. Opening it, he saw it was stuffed with twenty dollar bills neatly arranged with all the faces to the front wrapped in red rubber bands. Under the envelope were several thick plastic sandwich bags with huge amounts of pills in each. Digging deeper, Little Ro discovered another brown paper bag with a couple of plastic tubes of weed and a digital scale. Not knowing what to do next, instinctively being from the hood, Little Ro tucked the bag inconspicuously under one of the hedge trimmers, tossed the worn tarp on the cart and used a few bungee cords and old clothesline to secure the items down.

"Hey boy!" The woman rudely shouted from out the rear window startling Little Ro. "Hurry up and get off my property. And there ain't no need to come back around here either. I'ma get a real company to do my landscaping from now on out, not some inexperience kid!"

"Yes M'am!" Quick to grant her wish, Little Ro began pushing the cart out the driveway with one hand and the lawn mower with the other. Sweat started to pour down his face and in his eyes as the summer sun beamed down. Turning back only once to see if anyone from Lamont's house would change their minds about the belongings the woman, who'd seem to have made herself boss, just insisted he take, Little Ro nervously took the side streets to get to his house. Preoccupied with what he'd just seen in the shed and now had hid on the cart, the teen totally forget about the other yards he was scheduled to cut.

Chapter Four

Rushing the push cart into the two car garage, he unfastened the cords to retrieve the duffle bag. Wasting no time Little Ro raced in the side door of his house and straight to his bedroom. Turning the lock with the skeleton key, he closed his blinds and took the envelope out.

"This has got to be a dream. I can't believe it. Twenty, forty, sixty, eighty, a hundred," he repeated thirty one times.

Too many, $3,100 dollars wasn't a lot, but in Little Ro's household, that was way over the total amount his weary mother, Tosha, who often volunteered to work double shifts and overtime, made in almost three months. Amazed with his sudden cash windfall he recounted repeatedly, Little Ro didn't pay any attention to the bags of multi shaded pills still in the duffle bag or the weed.

"I'm gonna give half of this money to Ma," he proclaimed out loud. "Then buy me a new pair of sneakers and another lock and chain for the garage."

After spending all afternoon with pen and paper stretching out $3,100, Little Ro finally heard his mother come home with his sister Janai trailing right behind. Before he could inform her about his blessing, not to mention the tragedy of Lamont's untimely death, he saw the look of despair plastered on her face.

"What's wrong, Ma?" he took two bags of groceries out of her hands and sat them on the dining room table.

"My job at that tired factory just issued layoffs, and as you can see, your mother was one of the lucky ones who won't be getting a minimum wage paycheck come next week."

Watching her ball up the pink slip and throw it into the trash, Little Ro knew that it was his cue to save the day so to speak. Dashing back in his bedroom he lifted his mattress, grabbing the three stacks of money.

"Hey Ma! Guess what?" he asked, returning to the kitchen. "I got good news and bad."

"Not now, Roland," she sighed fighting back the tears from getting yet another disappointment from life. "I forgot the sauce for the spaghetti. Can you please run down to the store and get a jar?"

"Yes Ma but-"

"Please, baby. Tell me when you get back. Your sister has to eat and I have a major headache."

"Not a problem Ma. I got you!" Tucking the wad of cash in his front pocket, Little Ro headed out the door and up the block to the store. Feeling like a millionaire, never having had that much money in his possession, despite owing it to Lamont's sudden death, he was still in high spirits. Just when Little Ro felt no one could rob him of his happiness, he bent the corner and ran smack into Salena Jackson; the woman his mother blamed for all of their misfortune. Much to Tosha's delight, Salena was now the proud owner of a new title. Instead of a hoodrat she was now the neighborhood smoked out crackhead.

Salena's son, Sean, who detested the embarrassment of being birthed by such a female, was there as usual trying relentlessly to get his mother off the street begging her to go home, but as fate would have it, she was not the slight bit interested in Sean or any of his bright life altering ideas. Ever since Roland Sr.'s murder in her home years prior and the neighborhood's longstanding residents following Tosha's warning, Salena was ostracized and ridiculed by everyone who knew her now as well as back then.

"Hey Baby Boy," Salena sluggishly slurred her words, not immediately recognizing Little Ro. "I know you want some of this right here?" She put her boney hands on her hips and shook her body in a circular motion.

"Naw, I'm good." Little Ro was five seconds short of throwing up in his mouth as he looked his dead fathers ex-mistress up and down thinking to himself what in the world his dad could've seen in this crackhead to make him cheat on his mother.

"You sure?" Salena squinted while trying to comb her dirty fingers through her tangled hair. "I don't need much."

"Ma, what's wrong with you?" Sean snatched her up by the elbow jerking her to the side of the doorway. "Is you all the way crazy or what? What is you doing? Stop it!"

"Get ya hands off me!" she yelled at her son as Little Ro disappeared into the corner store. "I could've got me a few dollars from him since you ain't giving me nothing to work with! And I know you got it!" She rolled her bucked eyes. "You out here hating on me and that boy was buying! I know you seen him staring at me!"

"Shut up! Dang!" Sean shook Salena again while slamming her against the store's concrete wall. "Do you even know who that was you were trying to push up on? Do you? Huh? Do you?"

"What difference do it make to you if he got some money to give me? You always running behind me trying to act like you my daddy or something!" Salena rubbed her shoulder. "I'm ya Momma!"

Sean shook his head with contempt. "Why are you always embarrassing me? Ever since I was a kid it's been the same thing! You need to get some help- maybe Rehab!"

"I don't need no help Sean! I need some money and that straight laced looking boy seem like he got some to give, so fall back!"

"Look," Sean demanded to his mother. "When he comes outside leave him alone and don't say nothing! You understand-nothing!"

"What's the big deal, Sean? Why you all up in my face about some fool?"

"You so high right about now, you don't even realize who that is."

"Whatever," Salena waited by the store's doorway hoping to hit the teen up for his spare change. "Who is he?"

"Well, that was Roland – Roland Mills!"

"Huh?" Salena paused asking in a surprised tone not sure of what her only child had just said.

"Oh now you wanna pay attention!" Sean, head lowered, turned around, walking off before his former classmate had the chance to come out the store and clown him. "You make me sick! I swear for God I wish you was dead sometimes. At least I'd be free!"

"Little Roland?" Salena said under her breath as she stared down at the pavement. She felt a bit of shame cloud her cracked out brain. "Are you sure?" she called out to her son who was on the move.

Sean put his hand up, dismissing his mother, without even turning around as he walked out of sight.

Standing to the side of the store's glass door, a jumpy Salena waited as patiently as she could for the son of her murdered ex-lover to come out so she could apologize for her off the chain behavior. Even though she had a monkey on her back the size of Texas and was craving to get high, Salena let potential sponsors pass by feeling that she at least owed the young teenager an explanation as to why she'd came onto him the way she did.

Eventually Little Ro appeared from behind the store's doors.

"Hello Roland." Salena tried unsuccessfully to rub her matted hair into a ponytail, straighten out her oil stained blue jean skirt and lick her dry lips. "Can I talk to you about something?"

"About what?" Little Ro twisted his face, shrugging his shoulder to the side in attempt to avoid Salena's filthy hands from touching him. "I already told ya crackhead behind I'm tight!"

"I just wanted to let you know I'm sorry for asking you what I did. If I would've known you was my Roland's little son, I wouldn't-"

"Your Roland? Are you serious?" The youngster stopped in his tracks, looked her up and down, judgmentally laughing loudly. "Those drugs you on must really have your mind messed up or something; stepping to me like that. Your Roland...get on with all of that!"

"All I meant was that I was wrong and ain't mean to disrespect you." Salena followed him half way down the block, still trying to plead her case as Sean shamefully watched from the steps of one of his associate's porch. "Your father was a good man and I really loved him. How is your mother doing these days? Is she okay? How's your sister?"

Little Ro was infuriated, trying his best to remain calm as Salena continued to painstakingly trail behind him. Carrying the white plastic bag packed with his mothers' spaghetti sauce as well as chips, pop and a few candy bars he'd purchased for his little sister, he finally lost control of his emotions and let his deceased father's ex-girlfriend on the side have it full throttle.

"Stop talking about my father and asking about my mother - okay! Everybody in the hood knows if it wasn't for you being such a selfish minded hooker, he'd still be alive!" Not in his usual character, Little Ro had no problem screaming at an adult. "So for real, stop bringing up the past talking about how much you loved him! Go somewhere and do what you've been doing for years; smoke crack and leave me and my family alone! We catching it bad enough!"

Momentarily standing on the corner taking stock of what was said as Little Ro angrily marched away; Salena was interrupted by the sounds of an old grey Ford Tempo blowing its horn. She glanced over as she held on to the stop sign pole. Luckily for the dope man who was waiting somewhere to get paid by any means necessary, the driver signaled for the drug addicted Salena to come and ride with him around the block in the alley for a few minutes before he had to go home, undoubtedly to his wife and kids.

I don't know who she thinks she is talking to me like I care what she has to say. Little Ro contemplated with each passing step he took. *I would tell Ma what she had the nerve to say, but things are already bad enough for her. And if she hears this, she liable to go back up there and beat the brakes off that crackhead.*

"What up doe?" Sean, with pants sagging, ran off the stairs catching up with his former classmate who didn't even slow down his pace. "Let me holler at you for a minute."

"Listen up..." Still rattled with mixed emotions from his encounter with Salena, Little Ro barely acknowledged her son's presence. "If this is about what I just said to your mother, she straight had it coming."

"Naw, Guy, I know she be bugging out most of the time. That's what I wanted to say." Sean pulled up his sagging jeans enough to keep them from falling down to his ankles as he walked.

Little Ro was relieved that's all he wanted. He didn't want or need any sort of trouble from Sean Jackson, especially because of his rumored blood in blood out affiliation with a local gang. "Oh okay."

"Yeah it's all that dope that got her acting the way she does; out here running with all these so called men. You know what I'm saying."

Feeling a small bit of sympathy for Sean, Little Ro slowed his pace back to the house where his mother, who was hard working and would never think of doing the despicable things that Salena did, lived. "Dang Man, I'm sorry things are so messed up for you, but-"

"It ain't nothing." Sean tried down playing his pain, but unfortunately wore the grave appearance of sorrow written all across his face. "That's how it goes sometimes. We can't choose our family."

"Hey, not to get into your business," Little Ro continued his strange unexpected conversation with Salena Jackson's son of all people. "But how come you don't attend classes anymore? I haven't seen you around school since sometime before vacation started."

"Come on now, Dude, you know it ain't no secret that them busters at school was trying to hold me back another year. And a Cat like me wasn't going for that. School just ain't for me," he reasoned with Little Ro. "Besides, with a moms like mine, a brotha gotta get out here and grind if I wanna eat. You feel me?"

Before the unlikely pair knew it, they were standing in front of Little Ro's house, met by an impatient Tosha standing on the porch. "Boy, come your behind in this house with that sauce. You know Janai gotta eat before she starts practicing for that recital of hers!" she fussed.

"Okay, Ma." Little Ro got an epiphany as he glanced downward at the bag in his hands that were stuffed with items he'd purchased with the extra dough that lined his pockets.

"Alright, Dawg, I see ya moms is calling you, so I'm gonna bounce. Good looking on understanding that ole girl situation."

If he'd been any other friend from school, Little Ro would've invited him in to have dinner with his family, but considering who Sean and his mother was, Little Ro knew that definitely wasn't happening. So instead, Little Ro had an alternative idea.

"Hey, again I'm not trying to step outta line, but are you busy tomorrow about noon? I've got a business proposition for you that might make us both some money."

Hearing the word *money* was all Sean, who was always tangled up in some *get rich or die trying* scheme, needed to hear. He confirmed that he'd meet up with Little Ro in front of the store at twelve o'clock sharp before heading off into the *something dangerous darkness* that was Detroit. Little Ro then ran up the steps, disappearing into the security of his home.

Chapter Five

Little Ro looked at the clock that was hung on an old rusty nail over the kitchen sink. Realizing that it was close to twelve he got anxious. Rushing his mother and sister out the house to spend the eight one hundred dollar bills he'd blessed them with last night after lying about it being an advance on some huge month long yard work at a local charter school, he paced the floor with anticipation as well as hesitation as to whether he was about to do the right thing. Looking at the wastepaper basket that still had his mother's balled up pink slip on the top, and judging from the way her face lit up when he handed her that money, he quickly decided he was definitely about to embark upon the right change of hustle. Even if he did issue the money he'd discovered out to her a small bit at a time, Little Ro knew that blessing would soon run out, then what for him and his financially struggling family?

Fighting with his conscious, before the usually rational thinking teenager could second guess himself, Little Ro bolted out the door and up toward the corner store.

At exactly twelve fifteen, Sean turned the corner wearing the same clothes he'd had on the evening before.

"What up doe?" Sean, overly wrinkled, greeted Little Ro.

"Nothing much," Little Ro replied, suspiciously looking around the store's parking lot. "For a minute, I thought you weren't going to come." He glanced at his watch. "But I need to show you something. Hold tight a second."

"Well I sure hope it's some money."

Sean had greed in his eyes as he watched Little Ro dig deep into the pocket of his neatly ironed navy blue Dockers. Pulling out what appeared to be a piece of paper towel folded up, Little Ro looked around once more.

"Dang, Dawg, you killing me acting all top secret squirrel!" Sean teased. "What's the deal?"

Little Ro paid no attention to Sean's jokes while he carefully un-wrapped the paper towel, scoping out his surroundings the entire time. "Do you know what this is?"

Sean was confused as he took one of the small tablets out the napkin Little Ro held, flipping it over on the side that was embedded with a symbol. "I don't get it," he laughed, moving out the way of some customers that were pulling up into the lot. "What fool don't know what these is? The question should be what your *Dudley*

Do Right self doing with some Ecstasy Pills? I know you not getting lifted are you?"

"Ecstasy...I thought that's what they might've been, but I really wasn't too sure." Little Ro confessed his naïve knowledge of drugs all together. "And of course, I'm not getting lifted!"

"Okay, well where did you get them from and real talk, do you got some more?" Sean's eyes were still filled with greed as well as now the sound of his voice.

"Do you feel like coming over my house?" At this point Little Ro decided it would be better to just show Sean the deal than to tell him.

"Yeah alright, just let me grab a juice and a bag of chips for breakfast first," Sean insisted before they made their way to Tosha's house. Immediately going inside the store, Sean bought his nourishment ASAP so Little Ro could show him what he was working with.

Within minutes of arriving at the empty house, Sean couldn't help but to stare at the family pictures, school awards hung on the wall and the overall warm home like atmosphere he yearned for growing up. Finally go inside of Little Ro's bedroom, Sean soon saw the several big baggies full of different colored ecstasy pills. He quickly reassured his 'new best friend' that no doubt at twenty dollars a pop they were about to be rich, even if they split the proceeds straight down the middle. After carefully counting each pill one by one, the newly formed partners in crime determined they had over $50,000 in clear 100% profit on Little Ro's desk that was staring them dead in their faces.

"$50,000Dollars - I can't believe it!" Little Ro shook his head at the value at what the evil smart mouth talking relative of Lamont's had given him. *If she only knew what I'm sitting on thanks to her!*

"Yeah Ro, that's 25 stacks apiece right?" Sean chimed in making sure the cut was going to be fifty fifty even though his first mind wanted him to snatch it all and run out the front door. However 25 flat was more than good with him, especially considering he hadn't invested a dime.

After that was agreed the only thing the two had to do was to organize their game plan and get to work on moving the pills as soon as possible. Knowing absolutely nothing about drugs or the world which they came from, Little Ro relied solely on Sean and his street expertise to figure out the pros, cons and the logistics of them successfully converting bags of tiny pills into cold, hard revenue without getting shot, robbed, arrested, or even worse, killed.

*****

Over the next passing month and a half, life for both teenagers changed at a rapid transforming pace. They had quickly established a long and loyal customer base, which was enabling a sudden heavy cash flow to come into their possession and make their once common *low key hood life* jump to almost being neighborhood overnight *ghetto superstars.*

From day one when Sean received a 911 call on his cell and set out to sling the first four pills of his share of the product to Tim-Tim and his boy who were having a party with a couple of females, who soon also became customers themselves, each young man proved how differently they were raised and what was most important to them in their small corner of the world.

Trips to the mall for expensive outfits for his little sister were at the top of the list for Little Ro as well as a new Android Touch and a solid gold chain with a huge diamond encrusted cross. Never even having the desire to own a pair of the latest Jordan's, especially since he knew full well his mother could never afford such an extravagance on her meager salary, Little Ro purchased three pairs and a track suit to go with each. Treating himself to fitted caps, a brand new Play Station along with every game he desired and a pair of iced out Cartier glasses, Little Ro felt like a miniature kingpin. The once wise minded kid, who now owned over six G Shock watches, was spending money like it was going out of style.

"Yeah let me get two pair of those True Religion jeans in a 34 and them Hollister t-shirts –let me get one in every color you got." Little Ro instructed the salesman in the upscale store usually reserved for ballers.

"Yes Sir, not a problem." Although the salesman was old enough to be Little Ro's father, he respected the ridiculous amount of money the teenager always spent at his store. It was no doubt in his mind, it was dope money the youth was throwing around, but oh well, his job was to move merchandise, not judge. After all, most of his clientele were doing something illegal for a living.

Buying his sister every dress she wanted and even her own clarinet, he felt like a Big Man. Little Ro, of course, hooked Tosha up with lavish gifts, including money for a down payment on a new leased vehicle. Even though the way he and Sean's unlawful product was moving and they'd be out soon and with no available connect or any leads on getting any more, Little Ro still felt he owed his mother some sort of temporary happiness. Though she'd not once questioned him on his out of the blue windfall of finances, Little Ro knew she had to know that doing yard work wasn't the result of his new gained wealth.

When he came home riding a brand new moped- she said nothing. When he got his ear pieced and started rocking a half a carat diamond stud- she stood mute. And even when Little Ro showed up late one night having just gotten a huge cross, with R.I.P. and his father's name tattooed on his upper arm- Tosha didn't bat an eye. It was as if it was business as usual.

With the burden of being a grown man before he was truly ready, Little Ro missed out on being a young boy; watching television, climbing trees and hanging out with kids his own age. No sooner than his fathers' corpse was lowered into the ground and the first pile of dirt was thrown on top, Tosha pressured him to fill the painful void in her miserable life.

Every penny he'd make; every dime he found and every waking free minute that was available, Little Ro would spend in effort to make his often depressed mother happy once again. For that he would give almost anything and selling Ecstasy pills was making that more possible. Even the risk of getting arrested didn't persuade him to stop.

Meanwhile Tosha did manage to get another job after being laid off, but she unluckily lost that part time gig after barely receiving her first minimum wage pay check. However, she didn't worry as much as she did the first time she got laid off from her factory job, because she knew her son would certainly look out for the family. Matter of fact, she was counting on it.

Little Ro, was far from stupid and figured that this was why his once strict mother naively chose to disregard his obvious change in behavior and personal appearance differences. Once school had resumed, Tosha even took money from her son to let him sleep in and cut class for the day without having to hear her nagging. Anyone who paid attention knew Little Ro's change in demeanor and negative attitude toward school could only point to one conclusion; Little Ro was now a true Detroit hood hustler.

As an unemployed, single mother of two, Tosha needed the money for past due bills. Not to mention ever since her husband's murder, the mentally anguished mom could now sit back and kick her feet up. Growing up in a huge family that was overly packed full of criminals, including backsliders, alcoholics, crackheads, murders and other relatives that committed all types of mayhem, Tosha purposely turned away from that lifestyle knowing the street life nine outta ten ended in one of two ways; dead or in jail. She'd seen the ugly side of the so called game by attending several family members' funerals as well as made her fair share of trips to visit her kin in prisons scattered all across Michigan, Indiana and Ohio.

Now sadly, Tosha herself had fail prey and was caught up enjoying fast money, ignoring the tangled strings that were always attached to it. It was true what was always said; Money does change people. As Tosha, once simple minded and easy to please started dressing good, driving good and eating good, how Little Ro was making that happen was no more than an afterthought. Tosha was content allowing her son to take a chance with his life and freedom for her own selfish pleasures.

*****

Sean Jackson, Salena's boy, however, was a horse of a much different color. While most would think he'd easily out shine Little Ro when it came to letting go of the almighty dollar, Sean held onto it tightly as if he'd himself lived through the Great Depression. Being a child of a crackhead, Sean knew all good things came to an end and their Ecstasy hustling run would ultimately be no different.

Despite being labeled street savvy and surrounding himself with plenty of dime piece females, Sean honestly didn't mind playing the background when it came to him and Little Ro's venture. Wearing the same three pair of pants he owned day in and day out was like second nature to the only child of a narcotic addicted single parent. Tragically, Sean grew up having nothing to call his own, not even his mother's love, which ultimately belonged to the unfeeling streets of Detroit and whatever man could afford her cheap services.

Even if a stranger showed pity on Sean as a small child, giving him something as insignificant to most as a pair of new Spider Man pajamas, cold heartedly Salena would steal them, getting whatever few pennies she could scrounge up for a hit. Now that he was older, Sean tried persistently to get his mother off the streets and into some sort of Rehabilitation Treatment- but no dice. The heavily crack cocaine and Wild Irish Rose wine addicted Salena would have no parts of it.

Secretly at night, when he was sure no one was watching, wherever he was lucky enough to lie his head down, Sean would drop to his knees, lower his head and pray to God to deliver his mother back to her right state of mind. *Dang I'm tired of her being messed up and people dogging me about the foolishness she do. Please help my mother be a better person.*

Sure, prior to the death of Roland Sr., Salena Jackson was considered the neighborhood tramp by most of the neighborhood, but in Sean's eyes, that insulting title was miles behind the one his mother held claim to now; a grimy dirty do anything for a dollar crackhead. If there was one good thing that came out of Sean's ongoing tormented ordeal of being Salena's bastard son, it was that the life he lived had made him stronger. Now in his opinion, everything was about to start paying off. If he just kept stacking his bread, he was gonna be on top, was all Sean stayed focused on, not jacking off money.

Chapter Six

"**H**ey, guy, everything seems like its moving good, don't it?" Sean counted out his share of the day's profit. Smiling from ear to ear he stuffed the tiny knot of mostly twenties and tens deep down in his pocket for safe keeping until he got to the place he called home to put it in his ever growing stash.

"Yeah, you're right." Little Ro rubbed the side of his face in the mirror over his dresser, eagerly checking to see if the beard he had started growing was getting any thicker.

Sean handed him his share of the cash and the two made their way towards the front door.

"I'm about to grab something to eat, hit the mall and then go to the movies with my girl," Little Ro bragged counting his money. "You wanna hang or what?"

"Naw- not me. I'm on my way in for the night." Sean shook his head as he walked onto the front porch of Tosha's house where he was now regularly welcomed with open arms.

Greed along with selfishness was now the head of Tosha's twisted household. And if her dead husband's mistress bastard son had anything to do with her new carefree lifestyle, then so be it. Sean Jackson was and would always have an open door policy with her. Caught up in 'getting hers', Tosha still tried avoiding as much contact with Sean as possible, but to keep the money flow, she'd roll with the punches letting bygones be bygones.

Tosha felt she'd paid her debt off in full to the world in the way of her husband being suddenly and cruelly snatched out of her and her children's lives. So if any one of her holier than thou neighbors, like old Mr. Martin or her nosey Auntie Bell had some smart remarks or opinions about how she was now raising Janai or Little Ro, then they could just kick rocks as far as she was concerned.

"Dang Sean, you don't ever go out and have a good time, do you?" Little Ro took his brush out his back pocket.

"Yeah, man, but right about now, I'm on a serious mission. I got real thangs to do and real moves to make. You feel me?"

"I understand all that, Guy, but honestly; we's making nice money now." Little Ro pulled out the small knot of money he intended on blowing on clothes and females later. "So why won't you buy yourself a couple of outfits and maybe some new sneakers?" He brushed his waves repeatedly.

"All that high priced crap just ain't for me right now. Besides every well runs dry and you know we running low!" Sean's mind thought about the small amount of pills they had left. "And it's not like we gonna re-up."

"Whatever, that's all good, but it still don't explain why you don't ever go out to the restaurant with me and eat good. In the past six or seven weeks, when I think about it, all I've ever seen you eat outside of the meals my old girl might cook if she's at home, is Campbell Soup, Vienna's Sausage and Spam. Now what's up on that? Dang, I know you got dough!"

"Listen, Fam," Sean reassured him opening the screen door stepping onto the porch. "Let me do me and you do you, okay. I already done told you I'm on a mission, so let's just leave it like that."

Little Ro followed him out the door letting his curiosity of the past finally get the best of him. Ever since the afternoon he and Sean decided to go into this *pill selling venture,* he'd avoided the painful link they shared from years ago. But, at this moment, something strange came over Little Ro and he couldn't resist the temptation of not bringing up the issue that drastically changed him, his little sister and his mother's lives any longer.

"Dawg, before you go, let me holler at you about something else." He placed his hand on Sean's shoulder. "I've wanted to ask you this for a good while, but real rap, I don't really know if I want to hear the answer."

Both sitting down on the front stairs, Sean braced himself also for the inevitable conversation he always dreaded having to have with his new found friend; the night Roland Sr., Little Ro's daddy and Tosha's cheating husband, was shot in cold blood in his mother's living room.

"I already think I know what it is." Sean lowered his head, hesitating to speak out of turn and hoping to just let sleeping dogs lay. "But go ahead and ask just so I'll know we're on the same page."

"Well, it's about my father." Little Ro confirmed exactly what Sean speculated the topic would be. "I know it's been years, but I need to know what happened that night. You know, the night my pops got killed. My mother cries almost every time somebody brings up that evening, so it ain't no way I can go and ask her. You feel me?"

"Yeah I do," Sean bit down on the corner of his lower lip.

"She wouldn't even let me miss school to go to the murder trial so I could hear first hand for myself what had gone down. She felt like I was to young back then to understand."

Although the last thing Sean wanted to talk about was that tragic night that also haunted him, he obliged Little Ro and did just that. Since his promiscuous mother was indeed truly to blame, he felt he owed him at least that much.

Only ten minutes or so deep off into the *back down memory lane* conversation, Little Ro felt himself grow more and more agitated at what he was hearing. His heart raced and his blood boiled just as if the murder was taking place right now in front of his face. He could remember so vividly wishing that evening in his prayers, his father would go away and never come back home. Consumed with emotions, closing his eyes, Little Ro could almost visualize his mother running out the house that night saying his dad had been hurt and him being left standing there speechless and full of guilt that possibly his wish had came true.

The story Sean told of that dreadful nightmare unfolded from his end. He started at the very precise moment his mother, who was getting slapped around placed that ill fated, help me, help me distress call to Little Ro's Pops. That was the phone call that led to the confrontation between Salena's other man, who'd just been released from the county jail and Roland Sr.; the confrontation that ended with the ambulance (Sean called) rushing Roland Sr. off to the hospital where he took his final breath.

After calling his wife, Salena Jackson had been right there clinging to Roland Sr.'s side, much to the un-liking of a hysterical Tosha who arrived at the hospital, bursting through the doors and pass security just in time to see them pronounce the time of *her* husband's death.

Just listening to the details of how Salena's other man had been beating on her and she had called his father over to the rescue, to be Superman, made Little Ro's adrenalin rise. *Why didn't Salena call the police? Why didn't Sean? Why did she have to call his father? Why did his father get up from the dinner table? Why was he thinking it was alright to cheat on his mother in the first place?* The more unanswerable questions he thought about sitting on the stairs, the angrier Little Ro got.

"You can stop," Little Ro loudly ordered Sean. He held his head down buried in his hands. "I'm tight! I don't even wanna hear no more."

"Dude, I apologize for the role my mother played in your father's death," Sean tried consoling his new friend and business partner even though he knew it wouldn't soothe his pain. "That scandalous mess she did that night is what got her so jacked up now and out her mind. They say God don't like ugly, so now I guess she getting paid back everyday out in these Detroit streets and me right along with her!"

Little Ro lifted his head slightly enough so Sean could see the redness of his eyes and the complete look of disappointment on his face. "Yo, I'm good. I just wanted to know what really jumped off."

Sean took that as his cue to get up and head to the crib. "It is one other thing. In case you wanna know," Sean added with compassion looking Little Ro eye to eye, "When the ambulance was taking him away, I heard ya old man pleading with my mother to call your moms and tell her he loved her and his kids. Despite what you think Ro, ya pops was a real stand up dude in the end."

"Oh yeah?" Little Ro, at that point, really didn't know how to take that last bit of information about his adulterous father, so he just nodded, lowering his face back down in his hands as Sean left.

Chapter Seven

I can't believe that! Why did I even let him tell me that garbage? Then he gonna lie and say my no good cheating father said he loved us! Yeah right! That's a joke. If he loved me, my sister and my momma so much, he wouldn't have been cheating on her in the first place, especially with that boney crackhead! Little Ro reflected on what he'd just heard, leaving himself numb to any type of respect for Roland Sr. or his legacy.

His plans for having a good time later were halted as he sat on the porch infuriated, not knowing what to do next. As he simmered shooting phone call after phone call to voice mail, he suddenly had the strange desire to not remember what Sean had put on his mind. It was only one way he could do that and it was to buy something to drink, after all it worked for his mother all the time. Whenever Tosha was depressed, which was often, facing the troubles of the world, that closet hidden bottle took the edge off and often seemed to put his mother in a much better and mellower mood.

I need to get drunk or good and buzzed for real. Slowly getting up brushing off his designer blue jeans, Little Ro headed down the block toward the corner liquor store where he was stopped by, of all people, Salena, who darted out the alleyway after trying to con some old man in a red Ford F-150 out his money.

"Hey now, Little Roland," Salena smiled showing her rotten teeth as she squinted. Having a flashback, of the good old days, before she'd begin worshiping the crack pipe, Sean's mother took notice of all the similarities and characteristics her once upon a time boyfriend Roland Sr. and his son had in common.

"Oh hey Ms. Jackson," Little Ro, hard as it was, tried giving her a small amount of respect since he and Sean were now in business together as well as friends. "How you doing?"

"I'd be doing a whole lot better if you could just spare me a little bit of change so I can get something to eat."

"Come on now, Ms. Jackson, I know your son got your pockets straight enough to get a sandwich, so go pull that hungry routine with the next mark buster. Besides, I'm not in the mood for listening to all that game you be trying to run okay?"

"Listen baby," Salena, now feeling like she and Little Ro were on good terms, placed her hand onto his shoulder. "Sean is stingy and don't be giving me no money. He think I'm gonna just blow it on getting high."

"And is he wrong?" Little Ro shrugged his shoulder backwards so her filthy hand wouldn't get his expensive Pistons throwback jersey dirty.

"Naw, but I'm a grown woman. I'm his momma he ain't mine!" Salena, already lifted beyond belief, clutched the five dollar bill she'd just worked for in the alley. "He can't stop me from doing what I do no matter how much he tries. Anyway, he ain't nothing but a hypocrite. I mean look at him running around here playing big bad dope man all week, and then trying to drag my behind to church with him on Sunday. He sounds like a fool!"

"What?" Little Ro paused not believing what she'd just said. Shocked as they continued to walk into the stores crowded parking lot, he responded. "Did you just say Sean be going to church?... Sean?"

"Yeah, I said church. Every Sunday now for a month or so he waking me up or be searching for me, thinking I'm going

Ms Michel Moore

with him. He even claims he's getting baptized this week. Ain't that about nothing?! Who do Sean think he is? He makes me sick sometimes!"

"Wow, that's deep," Little Ro replied laughing to himself trying to imagine big bad, I'm so cool, nobody can beat me, Sean, posted in church like he used to be when he was younger. "But, hey right about now I need for you to do me a small favor. Can you hook me up?"

"Anything for you," Salena was elated Roland Sr.'s son was coming to her for assistance. Normally in the world she lived in and the seedy circles she traveled, it was common knowledge that when anybody wanted anything from her, they had to pay for it. But of course, she would do anything to help out Little Ro anyway she could. "What you need, Angel Face – looking just like your daddy?"

Letting her get away with even mentioning his father, especially with the black hearted Detroit State of Mind he was in, Little Ro reached into his pocket pulling out a crisp fifty dollar bill and handed it to Salena. "Look, I need for you to go in the store and buy me a drink- some Remy."

"You want a drink?" she couldn't believe what the once goody two shoes had said. "Did you say you want some Remy? Naw... not you Little Ro? What happened to that nice-"

"Yo listen Salena, you can kill all that extra noise," once again he was thrown back to disrespecting her and her drug addict lifestyle. "You can spare me all them judgmental stares and trying to be all up in my business! Just do what I asked you! Besides, you the last one that need to be around her acting like you anybodies mother! And, oh yeah, after you cop that bottle, you can keep the change, so you can do what you do!"

"Good looking Sweetheart, say no more. Momma Salena got you!" Bobbing her head scratching at her arms, Salena happily went into the store so that she could cop Little Ro's poison for comfort, a bottle of liquor and soon after, with the change he so graciously was allowing her to keep, she would cop the poison of her choice as well, crack cocaine.

*****

What seemed like hours slipped by as Little Ro, who admittedly was not a drinker, attempted to drown his sorrows by nursing the Fifth of Remy Salena had purchased on his behalf. Throwing rocks at his mothers' empty flower pots, which served as perfect targets, the young man sat posted on the third step from the top yelling out from time to time, obscenities and cursing the name of everybody who he felt was responsible for his father being snatched out his life; including Salena, Sean, his mother Tosha for nagging his pops like she used to and his old man Roland Sr. for being so dumb, selfish and stupid to put the next woman and kid before his own.

Little Ro was confused and his emotions were running wild. *I hate my father! I hate him and everything about him!* Echoed throughout his mind, consuming him with an intense fury and rage he had never felt before. *I'm glad that disrespectful bastard is dead! Good riddance! I hope he's burning in hell!*

Several of Tosha's long time neighbors came onto their porches to see what all the commotion was about at the small framed house that was normally quiet- that was up until lately. Gossiping amongst themselves, they'd all taken notice of Little Ro's now increasingly blatant and sometimes rude behavior, but dare not bring the unexpected change up to Tosha pertaining her precious baby boy's demeanor especially considering she seemed to be suffering from the same wild unpredictable transformation in her own lifestyle. The pair was both keeping late hours, had strange cars stopping by at all times of the night, and not to mention Little Ro hadn't volunteered to cut their yards in weeks.

Tosha Mills used to speak every morning she went to work or share a cup of coffee, but now as the nightclub hopping single mother of two drove by in her new truck she scarcely acknowledged her long time neighbors that stood by her when she and her kids were down and out. Maybe she was blinded by all the short dresses, tight jeans and flashy jewelry she'd been rocking the last couple of months. Those things were hindering her once sensible judgment was the sentiment of most. Possibly that's also why they hadn't seen that much of her daughter Janai lately and Tosha condoned the twisted reality of Little Ro keeping company with the likes of Sean Jackson and that no good shady mother of his, Salena.

Seeing the young man was distraught and obviously troubled, old Mr. Martin, who was pushing seventy one decided to take action. Out of concern, he held on tightly to the black steel handrail making his way off his porch and across the street to console his former friend and Masonic Lodge Brother Roland Sr.'s son. "Hey now," he smiled reassuringly like he had so many other times throughout the years. "Do you need to talk to someone?"

"Naw, Mr. Martin. I'm good." The teen's breath reeked of liquor as he stood to his feet, almost losing his balance. "I'm real, real, real good!"

"Well you don't look good Son. Why don't you come on over to my house, put that bottle down and let my wife fix you a plate of that good home cooking of hers you like so much."

"I pass," he slurred.

Not ready to give up on Little Ro, Mr. Martin tried insisting, hoping he'd change his mind. "Come on now, a hot meal will do you good. It's smothered pork chops and mash potatoes."

"Naw, I done told you once, I'm okay." Little Ro tried stashing the half smashed bottle of Remy behind one of the flower pots as he wildly waved his arms, dismissing the elderly Mr. Martin. "You can go on and just leave me alone. I don't need nobody's help! I done told you- I'm good!"

"Alright, alright, alright." Mr. Martin reached in his back overall pocket and got out a handkerchief wiping the sweat from his brow. "I'm gonna do just that, son, because I see that you are intent on going down the road of self destruction and defiance. But while you taking that hard, bumpy and unfortunately traveled often journey, take these words of wisdom along with you for comfort. Remember son, it ain't never too late to turn back on that road and do the right thing."

The last thing Little Ro wanted to hear about was doing the right thing. "Mr. Martin, go on back to your house and leave me alone! And stop calling me son! You ain't my daddy!" He demanded falling back onto the pillar knocking one of the flower pots to the pavement. "I ain't got no Daddy! He ain't care about me or my momma! He left me! You act like you wasn't around back then! You know what he was doing!" Little Ro pointed around at all the other seemingly concerned long time neighbors outside. "Y'all all knew!"

"Yes, son, that's true, I'm not your father, but remember this," Mr. Martin preached with a tone of certainty in his voice. "If you trust in the Lord, He'll never abandon you. And as for Roland Sr., I bet my last dollar he's up in heaven missing you every passing day. So try to be the best you, you can be and make him proud. You owe it to yourself."

With his spontaneous fiery filled sermon concluded, Mr. Martin, went back to the security of his front porch. Little Ro licked his lips and leaned back, reaching for his bottle, defiant in the advice he was just given. Twisting the cap off, raising it to his lips, he glanced down at the bottom stair as he took another long swig. "Who do that old man think he talking too? Trying to tell me what I need to be doing! I'm gonna be a boss one day selling those pills! I'm the man - a way better man than my dead daddy ever was!" he mumbled under his breath.

Mr. Martin watched the young troubled teen from his porch and shook his head wondering what was gonna become of Little Ro if he kept on the path he was traveling. *One day that boy gonna learn, I just hope it don't be too late.*

Chapter Eight

On his second trip to the store, a totally wasted Little Ro tried and tried, but couldn't find Salena to do him the same solid she'd done earlier by buying him another bottle. Barely standing against the brick wall of the stores' parking lot, he attempted coaxing person after person, no matter who they were, in hopes that one of them would be dishonest and dumb enough to break the law and risk getting ticketed to buy his under aged already drunk self some more liquor.

"Hey you," Little Ro belched out loud as his eyes darted around the crowded street. Cocky he waved another fifty dollar bill in the air. "Hey man, can you grab something out the store for me? Can you look out for me?"

"Naw Young Playa," one guy responded dressed in suit and tie.

"Ain't that Tosha Mills' son?" another one commented to her friend as they walked pass. "It's a shame how these kids behave when they raise themselves. Look at him, drunk as a, I don't know what. He ain't a thing like his daddy used to be."

"Girl you right," the other woman replied. "I know that man turning over in his grave; his wife out here running the streets like she young again and his son drunk as a skunk."

Hearing people ignore his demands and then talk about him and his mother like he wasn't there and on top of that, comparing him to his two timing, cheating, womanizing father, Little Ro grew more enraged than he was when he'd first walked down the block. His small frame shook and his jaws grew tight.

"Y'all don't know me or nothing about me," Little Ro shouted out so the entire world could hear him. "I'm sick and tired of y'all hypocrites trying to judge me! I'm my own man! I make my own rules!"

As Little Ro stood in the middle of the parking lot, jeans sagging, proclaiming his independence and manhood, two plain clothes police officers pulled up. After receiving a call from the stores' owner who'd got complaints from several older customers about a teenager outside disrespecting them, they observed the youth briefly before getting out of their unmarked vehicle. Trying his best to refrain from any more outburst as they cautiously approached him with their guns drawn, Little Ro let the liquor take back over his system, resulting in him cursing them out without any regard whatsoever for their authority.

"Y'all can beat it, ya feel me? Ain't nobody scared of y'all cause y'all got a badge and a gun! Everybody in the hood got a gun- even me! So get on!"

As if matters couldn't get any worse, one last sign that Little Ro shouldn't have be drinking jumped off as he violently vomited all his stomach's contents on one of the officers' shoes and down the front of his expensive jersey as they slammed him down against the concrete pavement, face first, checking the wild youth for any weapons or drugs.

Struggling with the police officers for a good solid minute or so, Little Ro, who was outnumbered and oversized by the two cops, finally stopped resisting and was thrown handcuffed head first in back of their maroon colored unmarked vehicle and quickly whisked off to the local precinct.

No sooner than they arrived at the station, still defiant, drunk and pissed off, the rebellious youth used his feet to repeatedly kick the car's rear window until it cracked. Fortunately for him, as luck would have it, the Desk Sergeant on duty recognized Little Ro from cutting his yard in the past and stopped his officers from any rough house retaliation that was sure to follow.

After logging in most of Little Ro's property that was on his person, the sergeant took notice of one particular item he wasn't used to seeing in the young man's possession; a few pills that seemed to be Ecstasy which was becoming increasingly popular with the youth their precincts officers had encounter recently.

"And just what are these pills here?" He firmly inquired.

"Aspirin," Little Ro wisely fired back. "I have Migraines real bad."

"Oh yeah...Migraines huh? Is that a fact?"

"Yeah it is." With his lip split, Little Ro stood his ground.

"Well it looks like Ecstasy to me." The Desk Sergeant fumed.

"Wow," Little Ro mocked. "You must be C.S.I. or something like that!"

Having had just about enough of the cat and mouse game he was playing with the arrogant teenager, the sergeant led a still heavily inebriated Little Ro over toward the black desk top telephones.

Making his one phone call, which was of course, to his mother since he was legally still underage, a dizzy Little Ro could hardly get the words out that he was arrested and being held at the Tenth Precinct before Tosha started screaming at the top of her lungs. Holding the telephone receiver as far away from his ear as he possible could, Little Ro closed his eyes, wondering how his life had gotten so far out of control in such a short time. Listening to Tosha's voice, which was filled with rage for her son interrupting her evening plans, made him want to throw up again.

It seemed to Little Ro, that in between now being totally responsible for paying all the various household bills and giving his Great Auntie Bell money to take care of his younger sister while his mom ran the streets trying hopelessly to recapture her youth, he was losing his mind. Finally hanging up the phone, Little Ro was glad to go to the holding cell where he could lay back and hopefully sleep off the sickness to his stomach and massive headache he was suffering.

*****

 Another police officer escorting Little Ro to his temporary home away from home was not as friendly or as reasonable as the Desk Sergeant. He, like the two cops that arrested him, had no problem whatsoever man handling the teen. Practically dragging Little Ro down the long dark mildew smell infested hallway, it was business as usually with him. The officer didn't know or care about Little Ro and his problems. To the Detroit Police Department, Roland Dean Mills Jr. was just another out of control juvenile throwing rocks at the penitentiary.

Shoving Little Ro into a small size bullpen with several other men would normally have made Tosha's naïve to the streets son be scared to death. Up until recently, the only type of contact the straight 'A' student was used to having with the police or criminals was watching episodes of Law and Order on television. If it wasn't for that bottle of Remy still flowing through his system and him wanting to throw up again, the wanna be tough teen would've been screaming for his mother. Instead, Little Ro man-ed up, taking a seat in the corner on a hard wood bench.

As he sat there trying to keep his composure together, Little Ro nervously wrung his hands repeatedly. Reading the various names that were scraped on the wall of the paint peeling holding cell to waste time, he soon was approached by a familiar face.

"What you doing in here Young Blood?"

"Oh hey," Little Ro didn't know the older guys name for sure, but he was used to seeing him all the time with Lamont. "What up doe?"

Smelling the youngsters breath made the man the streets had nicknamed, Keys take a couple of steps back. "That's what I was about to ask you. The last time I saw you over my people house, you was looking like a school boy- all tight and what not."

"Yeah school," Little Ro slurred. "Forget school!"

Confused, Keys shook his head. "Oh yeah, well dig this. I heard you got all that lawn 'equipment' and what not out the back shed."

"And?" Little Ro still felt a bit of liquid courage aggressiveness that he needed to get off his chest. "A lady at the house said I could have it. I didn't steal it!"

"Yo fall back killer," Keys laughed at the young teen that barely filled his torn jersey. "My sister Tanika told me what was jumping off over there that day after my manz got murdered. I ain't mad. I'm just saying you looked like you done stepped up your game. How that 'equipment' been working out? You good?"

Little Ro calmed down knowing Lamont's friend meant him no real harm, but he had to have known about the duffle bag and its contents he'd found that afternoon. "My bad, I'm just going through some stuff right now."

"What you doing in here? Why you get knocked?"

"All I was doing was trying to get somebody to buy me another bottle and then the police showed up tripping."

"Oh is that all?" Keys made two guys that were sitting on the bench ear hustling move to the other side of the cell. "I thought it was that 'equipment."

Realizing the kind of clout Keys had amongst the prisoners in there made Little Ro start to feel like he could spend the night, no problem, if his mother decided to teach him a lesson as she had threaten on the phone. "Yeah, that's all." He acted like he hadn't heard him mentioning the 'equipment.' "My mother said she's coming to get me when she leaves the casino so-"

"Your mother," Keys smiled. "I wish it was that easy for me to call my mother. Boy you don't know how good you got it. My Moms been dead ever since I was nine. I done got kicked out three foster homes, spent a year in juvenile and now I'm about to jail it this time for at least a twenty piece."

"A twenty piece?" Little Ro was lost on what Keys, obviously a seasoned criminal meant.

"Twenty years- a twenty year bid fool!" One guy shouted out who was obviously still listening.

Keys mean mugged the dude daring him to say another word. "Listen up. I ain't nobody's daddy or nothing like that, but somebody needs to put you up on some game and kick some real knowledge to you. And since my manz Lamont is gone and you was his people, I'ma keep it a hundred with you."

Little Ro leaned back paying attention, seeing that Key was done playing.

"That bag you was blessed with was nothing. Me and my crew get down like that all the time, that's why we let you keep your little come up. Trust, we had other things on our plate to deal with after Lamont got murdered." Keys grinned looking directly in the teenagers eyes sensing fear. "We let you bang School Boy because I thought you was trying to get college fare up or something, but you out here getting tangled up."

"But-"

"But nothing. Your mother about to come get you and when she do; make sure you don't end back up in here with the rest of us clowns. Trust me, being locked up like an animal for stuff you could easily avoid is the wrong move to make." Keys cracked his knuckles thinking about the various crimes he'd committed over the years. "Go to school and be a lawyer and come help me get up out of here! You still have a chance to change!"

Tired of hearing all of the 'you need to change' speeches, Little Ro was relieved when an officer finally came, calling out his name.

"Yo remember what I said," Keys walked him to the front of the cell. "And hold up. What size shoe you wear?"

"A ten," Little Ro answered while wondering why.

"Oh yeah, me too," Keys placed his hand on Little Ro's shoulder. "Before you go, I'ma need those new Jordans you rocking. I was locked up fighting this case when they came out. So run 'em. You don't mind do you? You free, you can always get another pair."

Little Ro wanted to tell Keys to kick rocks, but he knew he owed him at least that much for not letting the other guys in there beast him out, possibly taking more than his new sneakers.

Before stepping on the other side of the cell, Little Ro turned back facing Keys who was towering over him. "Hey, what you about to do twenty years for anyhow – I mean a twenty piece?"

"For killing the dude that killed Lamont. Not only was he my nephews father he was my best friend and trust good friends is hard to come by!"

"What?"

"You heard me, now remember what I said earlier! Don't let me see you back on this side again!"

Before another word could be spoken, the officer yanked Little Ro by his shirt leading him out the door.

Chapter Nine

It had been less than an hour and a half later, when assumingly concerned parent Tosha Mills pulled up in the police station parking lot. With designer purse on her arm, neck full of gold jewelry and nails perfectly manicured, she stormed through the doors of the building yelling out obscenities and cursing. "This don't make no kind of sense! All the crime going on in this city! The police need to out looking for murders or these carjackers out here, not arresting people kids that had something to drink!"

"Can I help you?" one annoyed officer asked.

Approaching the main desk with a serious attitude, Tosha boldly demanded to see her son and the officers that arrested him, causing her to leave the Casino earlier than she'd planned. "Yeah, I'ma need y'all to release my son Roland Mills Jr. and I wanna see the bored cops that ain't have nothing better to do to earn that city paycheck my taxes go to!"

It was obvious to the officers on duty that Tosha was the young boy's mother because that apple definitely didn't fall far from the tree. Little Ro was rude, disrespectful and obnoxious earlier, just like she was behaving now. How they saw it, her and the boy both needed some sort of counseling or family therapy in their lives.

The Desk Sergeant shook his head. He was still amazed, after all his years on the job, how some so-called parents acted when their children broke the law. It was as if they were mad at the system for catching the little heathens rather than being mad at their child for being a heathen.

"Yes, are you Roland Mills Jr. Mother?" the sergeant knowingly inquired.

"Yes, I am. Why else would I be down here asking about him?" she loudly and sarcastically stated. "Where's my son at and what exactly did you pick him up for, cause I know it couldn't be because the boy took a drink?"

"Well, there are several charges pending against him; Public Intoxication, Disorderly Conduct, Resisting Arrest and Destruction of Police Property."

"Oh naw! All of that?" Tosha frowned as he went down the long list she knew her baby wasn't guilty of. "Not my son, I don't believe it!"

"Sorry, Miss, but he is facing serious charges and his bond is rather high. Do you often allow him to drink? You know he's underage!"

"First of all, I know how old my son is, I gave birth to him! And secondly-a bond," she quizzed, planting her hands firmly on her hips. "Can't you just release him to me and stay out of the way I raise mines?"

"I wish it was that easy, but unfortunately it's not." The Desk Sergeant looked over his wire framed glasses. "He has to post a bond."

"Yeah well, I ain't in the mood for anymore speeches or impromptu parenting classes, so let's get on with it! How much is it then?" Tosha fumed as she opened her purse, ready to get out of there as soon as possible and hopefully back to the Casino where she was on a winning streak at the blackjack table.

When it was all said and done, Tosha, infuriated to say the least, counted out $3,500. Two thousand of which she had in her purse, one thousand in small bills Little Ro had on his person, and lastly five hundred dollars she withdrew out the ATM that was located at the corner of the block. Waiting an additional forty-five minutes to an hour for the paperwork to be completed, Little Ro, still sick to his stomach, was finally freed. Seeing his shirt was ripped and he had red marks on his face, not to mention a busted lip, Tosha swore she was going to be pressing police brutality charges on both officers for their treatment of her innocent teenage son.

Settling into the passenger seat of the Range Rover, sympathy definitely was not on Little Ro's side as Tosha read him the full blown riot act. She informed her son by the time she got home from gambling at the casino, she wanted every single penny of the bond money she'd just put up on her dresser waiting or it was gonna be pure hell to pay.

She's acting like I didn't give her that money in the first place or the dough for this truck. But I can't take hearing her mouth! I swear I can't! Little Ro muttered to himself. Suffering from a pounding headache, he felt like throwing up again with each pothole Tosha seemed to be purposely riding over and every corner of the Detroit streets she bent.

"How much was the bond anyway?" Little Ro sheepishly asked his mother.

"You owe me twenty-five hundred," she spat tossing the paperwork on his lap.

"Dang!"

"That's right dang! Twenty-five hundred and trust like I said, I want every penny back - ASAP!"

Little Ro didn't even think he had that much money in his stash considering the way he always blew his money pretty much just as soon as he got it. *I knew I shouldn't have bought that dang chain two days ago or those new games,* he fussed at himself. *And especially the new bracelet for her ungrateful self!*

Little Ro had to think quickly about how he was gonna get his moms her money back and fast. Most of Little Ro's customers were young kids from the high school, but he didn't have time to wait around for them to come to him. Although it wasn't something he particular cared to do, he knew that tomorrow he would have to go up to the high school and push all the pills he could to keep Tosha off his back.

As he continued to think where he could get the money from his mind kept flashing back to Keys and the advice or rather warning he'd given him.

Chapter Ten

Salena was good and toasted. After purchasing the bottle of liquor for Little Ro, she had over thirty five dollars left. Having bought a bottle of wine for herself and spending the rest on some crack, she was happy. Feeling like nothing could blow her high, she sat back quietly letting her son tell her all the reasons she was an unfit parent.

"How many times do I have to tell you to stop using that garbage?" Sean frowned watching his dazed underweight mother lay across an old couch. "You don't eat anymore, you don't bathe and you ain't washed your hair in months. It's obvious you don't care about me, but at least you could try caring about yourself again."

"Whatever Sean. Leave me be."

Going into the kitchen of the sparsely furnished studio apartment they had moved into illegally, Sean came back to the room with a bowl of Ramon Noodles. "Here Ma, at least eat some of this to soak up some of that cheap wine you got in your system."

"I ain't hungry, now go on somewhere and leave me alone unless you talking about giving me some more money." Salena demanded staggering to her feet.

"That crack got you gone enough." Trying to force the issue, Sean held the bowl of the chicken flavored poor man's feast up to his mothers' nostrils. "Just taste a little bit."

"Naw Sean, I ain't interested."

Disappointed he couldn't make Salena try to sober up so he could talk to her like she had some sense; Sean lost his temper all together. "I'm done with you. Do whatever you want from this point on; smoke crack, drink yourself stupid, run the streets to the sun come up and go down again."

"I don't need you no more," Salena got loud with her son. "Little Ro got me."

"Little Ro," Sean sat the bowl of noodles on the table. "What you mean he got you?"

"Don't worry about what I mean."

"I know he ain't give you none of that work!"

"I don't want none of them pills y'all boys got."

"Then how he got you then?"

"None of your business, but just know Little Ro and me is tight now. We got our secrets!" Salena smiled showing her yellow teeth.

"Okay then, we'll see how tight y'all is," Sean stormed out the door.

Dang, I swear I don't wanna hear her mouth whenever she gets home! Why did I jack all that dough on stupid stuff? Little Ro paced the floor persistently in hopes of coming up with an immediate solution to ensure Tosha wouldn't be on his back about her money. His plan to go up to the school and push some pills failed miserable. Apparently it was a bomb scare and extra security was called in to patrol the inside of the building and the outer perimeter. The high school was on total lockdown. There were a couple of suited up security guards that had everybody noided, including Little Ro. He felt it best not to push his luck. The last thing he wanted to do was end up in jail again and owe his mom's even more money, that is if she would take any more time out her hectic 'good time' schedule and even show up to bail him out. Plus he didn't want to run the risk of running back into Keys before he got shipped upstate to the penitentiary.

Craving another drink to fight the demons that filled his head, Little Ro retrieved a bottle of Absolute his mother kept on the top shelf of the kitchen cabinet behind her good set of dishes for so called emergencies. *I need this right here so I can figure this madness out.* Twisting the top off, taking it to the head for a quick swig, he was stopped by a series of hard knocks at his front door.

Bam, bam, bam, bam. The thunderous barrage of bangs increased. *Bam, bam, bam.*

"Yeah, who is it?" Little Ro, still buzzed from the night before and not thinking clearly, grabbed a pistol he kept tucked underneath the cushion of the sofa. Gripping up on the small size hair trigger revolver he'd traded a few pills for to a desperate customer from the Suburbs, he took a deep breath asking again, "Yeah! Who that?"

"Yo, it's me Dude." Sean pounded his fist against the wood door once more as if he was the Detroit Police Department, causing the frame to rattle. "Open up!"

Realizing who it was Little Ro set the gun that made him feel tough, on the mantle above the fireplace right next to an old family portrait taken back when his father was still alive and life was simple. He then turned the knob, letting his homeboy into the house. "What up, doe?" he slurred to some extent, nodding his head upward.

"Hey Ro, did you give my ole girl some money before you bugged out last night, getting yourself arrested?" Looking his friend in the face, Sean, visibly livid, wanted a straight answer. "Because she tripping."

"Naw I didn't, why you say that?" Little Ro, who was far from being in the mood or mindset to care about anything dealing with Salena and her ghetto mess, took another swig of the bottle of liquor.

"Because she got enough bread from somewhere to get high as three kites and she keeps mumbling something about you and her and some big top secret- acting like y'all buddies."

"Ah, Dawg, maybe before - when she copped me some Remy and I let her keep the change." Little Ro nonchalantly recalled as though it wasn't a big deal.

"Why you do that?" Sean, out of nowhere, lunged at Little Ro, yoking him up knocking the bottle out his hand. "That was foul!"

"Get off me! Is you crazy or what?" Little Ro shoved him back then straightened out his shirt he'd just taken the price tag off of earlier."Why you going all in like that?"

"I'm sorry, guy, but I've been trying to wean her off that stuff and convince her to get some help, maybe go to Rehab," Sean regained his composure. "So when she said *secret*, I knew she must've hit you up for some loot or pills or something."

Little Ro reached down picking the bottle off the floor, then took another sip. "You want some?" He extended the Absolute to Sean as sort of a peace offering.

"Naw, I gotta get back to the crib and make some phone calls about this house

Ms Michel Moore

I'm trying to get. Besides, you need to put that mess down. You already jacked up enough!" He pointed making reference to Little Ro's split lip and bruised face courtesy of the altercation with the cops. "The last thing I need is you and my Moms high!"

"Oh Sean, I get it - so you my daddy now too huh?" Little Ro thought back to old Mr. Martin, from across the street, trying to tell him what to do with his life just hours prior as well as Keys.

Sean was trying his best to remain calm, but was seconds from losing it again. "Look Ro, I'm just trying to put you up on game alright? I already done been down that drinking all day, tripping all night road. You messing up big time, that's all I'm saying."

"Well so what Sean-you ain't me!"

"I know I ain't you, but- "

"Yeah, but I just been through hell on earth!" Little Ro smiled, realizing a quick solution to his money woes. "But you can help ya boy out until next week."

"Help you out?" Sean paused. "With what?"

"I'm gonna need to borrow some cash real quick to repay my Moms for that bond she had to post. You know how she be acting about her money!"

Sean, who'd been on a mission of stacking dough since the day he and Little Ro linked up, didn't waste any amount of time stopping that notion from growing. "Look, I wanna work with you, but I ain't gonna be able to do it. Now I gotta bounce and make them calls. I'm out!"

"Whoa! It's like that?" Little Ro took a huge gulp, giving him more courage than usual as he tossed the still open bottle across the room, spilling the liquor out onto Tosha's new plush carpet. "Dawg, I know you got it! You ain't spent no money since day one, especially on clothes." Low key he dissed Sean about his appearance.

"And what's your point about what I do with mines?" Sean replied.

Little Ro, who was once intimidated by Sean and the rough street life he lived, had no problem whatsoever stepping to his supposed friend. "My point is if it wasn't for me hooking you up from jump, you'd probably be still up there on the corner with that tramp mother of yours-broke!"

Sean knew after what he'd told Little Ro about his pops murder, he was in a bad way. That's probably why he had all of a sudden found a new friend in the form of alcohol. So he tried harder than he normally would to overlook his disrespectful statements.

"Look Ro," Sean attempted explaining, "I'm saving all my money so I can rent a crib out in the Burbs and get my mother out this neighborhood along with all the horrible memories that haunt her and me every day. It's been hard for both of us over the years living around here and now..." Sean continued to let Little Ro know why he wouldn't and couldn't afford to loan him any money, especially the way Little Ro let money slip through his fingers like water. "I almost have enough money saved and you know we're almost out of product."

"It's been hard for y'all?" Little Ro interrupted and stepped back not believing what his boy had just said. "For real though, it's been hard on y'all? If it wasn't for your mother being so hot in the pants seducing my dad back in the day, he'd still be alive and things wouldn't have been so hard pressed on me. I've been the man around here since the night my ole girl came home from the hospital with my father's belongings covered in blood! And P.S., no matter where you take your momma, she always gonna be nothing more than a slime ball crackhead!"

"You know what; I'm gonna pray for you." Sean flipped the script coming out of left field with his response. "Going to church helped me not be so angry and it can help you too. It can help you change because you need to get your act together!"

"Look dude; been there done that! The only thing that's gonna help me is that money I need to give back to my mother. So I'ma need for you to run that bread and not your big mouth!" He yanked forcefully on Sean's arm then swung on him, hitting his friend dead in the jaw.

Having no choice but to defend himself Sean fired back, delivering a strong upper cut blow to Little Ro's midsection un-doubtfully fracturing a rib. The harsh hit he suffered caused the inebriated teen to get weak and wobbly in the knees. Sean then followed the first punch up by a clenched fist in Little Ro's left eye. As chaos and pandemonium broke out inside Tosha's house, the neighbors heard the loud commotion spill out into the street and called the police for assistance.

Consumed with not disappointing his mother, whom he'd die for, Little Ro gathered his self-control and composure. Wasting no time, he bulldog charged at his friend once more, not wanting to take *no* for an answer. Enduring three additional swift socks in his face and landing on the floor near the fireplace, Tosha's physically worn out, beat down son saw no other alternative as he reached up on the mantle grabbing his pistol.

"Real rap, I said run that money," Little Ro repeated with fury in his tone from the floor. "I'm trying to keep it a hundred with you! My Momma needs it! Sean, I ain't playing with you no more, run it!"

"For what Ro, so she can gamble and ride around in that new truck like she better than everybody else that live in the hood?"

"Well if she does, it's sure in hell better than smoking crack running behind every dude that got a dollar in his pocket and sleeping with the next woman's husband cause she couldn't find one of her own!" Little Ro held his injured side with one hand and the gun with the other. "Matter of fact, where is your father at anyway, or do Salena even know who he is?" He stood to his feet grinning as the alcohol kept his words slurring. "Now give me the money you got on you, my Moms needs it!"

"Dawg, your mother ain't no better than mine despite what you think or say." Sean hyperventilated while staring down the barrel of the gun. "And my Moms needs the money too!" Sean took his chances bum rushing Little Ro, which resulted in both of the troubled teenagers crashing on the oak framed coffee table then rolling around in the sharp pieces of the shattered glass top. Taking turns being on the bottom, both suffering from deep cuts, the inevitably finally happened.

Bang, Bang!

The loud ear deafening sounds of the revolver being fired twice echoed throughout the house as Sean and Little Ro both lay motionless on the floor; one in shock of shooting his friend and one in shock of being shot. As the multitude of police sirens roared in the distance, getting closer, neither teen moved a muscle. Minutes later, but what seemed like an eternity to the boys, Tosha's house was swarming with police, including the same cops who'd arrested Little Ro the evening prior. After a short while, gawkers who'd gathered across the street watched the ambulance technicians sadly bring out Little Ro on a stretcher barely clinging to life.

Having placed a call to his long time neighbor, recently ex-church member, Tosha Mills, informing her there had been some sort of altercation at her home involving her son and Salena Jackson's son, with Bible in hand, Mr. Martin quietly prayed for the injured youth as well as the shooter.

Sean, badly cut up from the glass he and Little Ro had rolled in, was totally distraught in a zombie like trance. As he was being handcuffed and led toward the squad car, everyone shook their heads. Word spread quickly of the shooting up to the corner store where Salena, as usual, was begging for money for her next rock. Rushing down the block to check things out with her only son and meal ticket, most of the folk standing around gave Salena cold hard stares of contempt like they had years ago after Roland Sr.'s death. Now they blamed her for the actions of her son.

"That boy didn't have a chance in life from the beginning." One woman hissed so Salena could hear.

"I'd probably shoot someone, then myself if I was cursed with a mother like her!" Another remarked.

A third person couldn't help but join in. "Yeah look at her trying to act all concerned. She'll be getting high on that crack rock no sooner than they bend the corner with that bad seed of hers!"

Ignoring the cruel judgments the slew of nosey bystanders were passing on her, as the squad car pulled off with Sean in the rear seat in tears, Salena asked one of the policemen still on the scene exactly where they were taking her underage son.

"By the looks of the victim and the amount of blood he's lost; your son probably is on his way to prison for the rest of his life." The officer nonchalantly replied.

Chapter Eleven

Here And Now

Lying on the stretcher, drifting in and out of consciousness while the doctor assessed his condition, Little Ro started to panic, realizing how serious his gunshot wounds were.

"Oh God! Oh God!" The numbness to reality caused by all the liquor he'd drank was fast wearing off. The pain became excruciating and almost unbearable to the teenager. "Somebody get my Momma! Get my Momma! Call her!" He squirmed from side to side as the nurses tried restraining him to put an I.V. in his arm.

"She's already here Son, so relax and let us help you!" the doctor bargained with Little Ro, who was just about his own child's age. "Just close your eyes and calm down while we do our job."

How did things turn out like this? God, please help me make it!" Little Ro prayed, feeling the pinch of a needle in his arm and a hot burning in the pit of his stomach. *"I don't wanna die like my father or Lamont! I wanna live!"*

For some strange reason, his thoughts stayed focused on Lamont and the day he found out he'd died and the nonchalant manner his family behaved as if his life didn't count for anything except for materialistic belongings. Little Ro didn't want to end up like that. He wanted to do something great with his life, something memorable besides selling pills to his classmates. He then remembered the words of Mr. Martin about making his father proud and Keys saying he should stay in school. Little Ro knew for the past couple of months or so he'd been living straight up foul, and if death was in the cards for him, then it was what it was and was gonna be what it be! He couldn't change that. It was now in God's hands.

However, one thing Little Ro knew for sure was, if he lived to see another day, the first thing he was gonna do was to tell Sean he was sorry for his part in everything that jumped off and he was a hundred percent right. No matter what mistakes Salena made, she was still his mom and she should come first in his life, like Tosha was top priority in his.

*****

Little Ro, fighting to survive, was in the triage area and then surgery for what seemed like hours.

"It just don't make no kind of sense to me. I swear you might as well just picked up that gun you allowed him to have and shot that poor child yourself!" The old woman repeated once more shaking her head at her niece's all of a sudden bad parenting skills and lack of concern for her children.

"Don't say that, Auntie Bell," Tosha shrieked, her voice echoing throughout the hospital. "I'm a good mother! I'd never do anything to harm one of my kids, so stop saying that!"

"You say that now, but you did harm him. Maybe not on purpose, but you still did. Forcing that boy to take his daddy's place and work every day after school. Then pressuring him all those times to keep his sister every Saturday instead of letting him be a normal teenager! Thank God I stepped in and took Janai when I did. Although now it looks like it might have been too late. But still, it was plain wrong, Tosha. There was no way that boy could fill a man's shoes!"

Tosha thought for a moment, taking in her aunt's judgmental words as she reminisced on how she handled things after the death of her husband, Roland Sr. "I never thought about it like that. I love my baby and just want him to be alright!" she continued to sob. Overcome with emotion and grief, Tosha's tears started to flow even more. She was almost hysterical when the unthinkable happened. Wiping her face she couldn't believe her eyes. "What are you doing in here? Who let you in?"

Not knowing what to do or say, Salena still heavily under the influence of drugs and alcohol, slowly walked toward Tosha and her aunt. "I don't mean to bother y'all, I promise, but-"

"But what Salena? What you about to tell me?" Tosha jumped to her feet wanting an explanation but really not expecting one. "You about to tell me you didn't mean sleeping with my husband or calling him that night he got killed? Or is you about to tell me sorry for that animal you raised up shooting my baby? Which one is it?" She didn't give a mentally unbalanced Salena a chance to respond as Auntie Bell pulled her back by the forearm. "Look at you! Roland Sr. was a fool!"

"Look, I don't want any trouble," Salena was attempting to come down from her high. "But they brought Sean here to treat him for some deep cuts and wounds he got in the fight and-"

Tosha broke loose from her aunt's weak grip. "Cuts! Are you seriously in here wanting some sort of sympathy because your boy got cuts? You best get on! I'm warning you!"

Auntie Bell had enough of the long standing feuding mothers focusing on the wrong thing and tried telling them just that. "Are you both crazy? Each of your sons has been out here doing wrong, breaking the law and y'all let them. And instead of trying to guide them in the right direction, leading by example, y'all in here fighting over something that happened years ago!"

Time and time again, Salena wanted nothing more than to approach Tosha and just apologize for what her selfish actions had caused to happen, but she knew Roland Sr.'s widow wasn't trying to hear it. Deep down inside she couldn't blame her.

"Naw Auntie Bell," Tosha couldn't be controlled or reasoned with. "First she killed my husband and now her boy tried to kill my son! She got me twisted!"

"Look at her Tosha," Auntie Bell demanded. "What else can you do to this poor creature that she hasn't already done to herself? And as for you Ms. Jackson, you need some serious help; it's a sin and a shame!"

Before the overly distraught Tosha could get an opportunity to swing on Salena, two police detectives entered the hospital waiting room wanting to question both mothers pertaining their sons and their recent illegal pill selling enterprise. After interviewing several residents on the block, they'd become aware of that activity as a possible motive to the shooting. The finger pointing and allegations had just started to fly when the doctor emerged out of the double doors and into the hospital's waiting area where his young patient's mother and Great Aunt were still there arguing with a remorseful Salena and the detectives about who did what and to who.

As he held a chart in his hands, Tosha bravely stood tall, preparing herself for whatever she'd have to face.

Salena, who had grew fond of Roland Sr.'s son over the past few months also hoped, for Sean's sake, Tosha's son would be okay.

"Hello, Mrs. Mills." The doctor took a deep breath as his patient's mother braced herself, holding onto her elderly aunt's arm. "It was touch and go for a good while, but fortunately we removed both bullets with a minimal amount of damage. It must've been Devine Intervention, because the bullets missed every vital organ. It might take a couple of months of your son being hospitalized to fully recover, but he's young and strong willed. He'll make it."

Tosha dropped down to her knees and cried out, "Thank God for giving me a second chance with my son and to make things right!"

"That's good news Mrs. Mills and we'll be back to talk to your son when he's up to it." One officer remarked.

"And as for you Ms. Jackson, when they finish up here with your son, Sean, he'll be transferred to the County Jail. More than likely he'll be charged with Attempted Murder." The other detective advised handing her his card. "Be grateful it could've been worse!"

Six Months Later...

"**A**lright Roland," Tosha stopped using the word 'Little' in front of his name and encouraged everyone else they knew to do the same. "Promise me you're gonna take it easy."

Getting out of the used vehicle his mother was now driving since turning in the Range Rover she couldn't afford after he stopped his illegal activities, Roland smiled while his sister climbed in the front seat. Reaching back inside for his cane, he kissed his mother on the cheek. "Mom, don't worry. I'm gonna be fine. Since you started back working you never have any fun. Maybe you and Janai can have a girl's night together watching movies or something." Still to some extent recovering from his gunshot injuries, Roland decided to get away from the 'hood' and spend the weekend in the quiet Suburbs.

Tosha smirked, knowing her son was now a man. Not because she needed him to be, but because it was time. "Okay, just don't push yourself too hard."

"He won't Mrs. Mills," Sean met his best friend at the curb helping him with his bag. "Besides going to church with me and my mother on Sunday, we gonna pretty much stay in the house so I can beat him on X-Box."

Tosha gave Sean a slight smile. "How is your mother doing anyway?"

"Great! Since moving out here, she's been off drugs for ninety seven days and counting!" Sean proudly announced, "Going to NA meetings and everything!"

Allowing her son to testify the awful shooting that took place at her home was indeed an accident and Sean was completely innocent of all charges that had been pressed, Tosha tried to make peace with the entire ancient beef she and Salena had. Although they ran in different circles and would never ever be friends, their sons were close, just like brothers and Tosha, out of love for Roland, grew to respect their bond.

THE END